GENESIS OF A VAMPIRE

ONE LOST SOUL WILL
SHAPE HUMAN DESTINY

Jon Finnwww.jonfinnauthor.com

Published by America Publishers

Book and cover America Publishers

June 2026

GENESIS OF A VAMPIRE

Beware reading this book invites
a vampire into your life. You should
never invite a vampire into your home.

Are you really going to invite
one in to your mind?

If you do, well done. You have
just signed up to a wild adventure.
Buckle up this is going to be fun.

REVIEWS

I love vampire books, not disappointed here. Stephanie (Amazon Customer, ★★★★★) Reviewed in the United States on 25 November 2025.

I bought this book because it is the beginning of a series, and I love vampire books. I was not disappointed. The book does a great job showing the tragic events that twist one soul into something immortal, transforming feelings rather than just supernatural. I liked the way the author blended ancient history, hidden secrets, and moral conflict. It made me want more. It's dark, thought-provoking, and sets up a series I definitely want to continue.

A Vampire story that feels fresh (Amazon Customer, ★★★★★) Reviewed in the United Kingdom on 20 May 2025.

This book grabbed me from the first chapter and wouldn't let go! The concept of a vampire who's been around since literal Biblical times is so fascinating. I love how Jacob starts as this sickly orphan in Nazareth (those conversations with teenage Jesus are wild) and then we follow him through major historical events as he pulls strings behind the scenes.

What makes this different from other vampire stories is how deeply it explores the moral struggles. Jacob isn't just some perfect, brooding hottie - he's genuinely conflicted about his nature and what he becomes. The historical details feel well-researched too, not just window dressing.

I devoured this in two days and immediately bought the sequel. If you're looking for a vampire series with actual depth and a unique premise, this is it. So glad I found this gem!

Captivating Book! Fun subject, interesting read (Amazon Customer, El mismo Che, ★★★★) Reviewed in the United States on 18 May 2025.

I really enjoyed reading this book! It flowed well and held my attention and was hard to put down. I found it captivating how Jacob's life began and how he developed into the vampire, not knowing he was or why he was different at first. Then how he planned the humiliation and retaliation toward his abuser. I'm looking forward to reading the next book in this series.

There won't be any spoilers here. "Genisis of a Vampire" by Jon Finn is definitely a unique twist on the vampire legend. It goes way back in history and seems to be a very good start to a series. Sharing the life journey of the main character in this new series, Jacob, will be interesting. Fans of supernatural historical fiction should find this an interesting read. Put it on your list!

The Beginning of a Fascinating New Book Series (Amazon Customer, Cubby Bear 1977 ★★★★★) Reviewed in the United States on 6 July 2025

This book is a strange yet intriguing story that begins a saga of an immortal vampire born during the time of Christ. This is an odd juxtaposition of characters whose moral compasses are sometimes at cross purposes. The book is the first of a series that chronicles the 2000 years of the life of Jacob, the vampire. Jacob begins his life in an orphanage, where he develops his morality through being bullied and seeking revenge, ultimately becoming a natural protector. However, due to his nature, he is also a murderer and a thief. The early interactions between Jacob and Josh(Christ) illustrate the complexities of their identities and friendship. This is a dark, unique fantasy and will appeal to both readers of historical fiction and horror stories.

Brilliant book. Amazon Customer, Kevin Street, ★★★★★ Reviewed in the United Kingdom on 15 April 2025.

I loved the Idea of this immortal Jacob travelling through time and sharing his adventures. As a Christian I am very interested in his relationship with Josh (Jesus) especially the years that are not mentioned in the Bible. Finn is a beautiful writer intertwining historical events with nuggets of wisdom in this thriller. I look forward to the next instalment and hopefully more about Jacob's relationship with Josh!

My latest read was Genesis of a Vampire, Book 1 of The Immortal Conquest Series, by Jon Finn, read on a Kindle. I thought the concept of this story was intriguing, an immortal vampire born during the time of Christ. This first book covers the main character,

Jacob's, time while living in an orphanage, finding himself as he deals with being a vampire, and befriending Jesus while they were children. The series will go on to cover over two millennia and the many experiences he lives through.

This first book's main story is mostly about revenge towards the orphanage bully, Paulius, though there aren't many examples of actual bullying behaviour.. Jacob also feels that he is a natural protector, though there aren't many examples of that, other than his revenge towards the bully. But then he, himself, is a thief and murderer. Jacob's friendship with Josh (Jesus) seems to be a side story, perhaps having more significance in future books in this series.

Haunting, Timeless Tale of Power, Blood, and Redemption! Tobi Sherbrook ★★★★★ Reviewed in the United States on 1 July 2025
This is not your typical vampire story; it's a sweepingly, deeply layered journey through 2000 years of human history, told through the eyes of an immortal soul burdened by power, pain, and purpose. Although a revision of the story expanded, it's a must-read for those who crave vampire novels.

CHAPTER I

The reverberations of the blows on the door echoed through the orphanage in a rolling thunder, shocking the staff nearest to the door. In the dormitory above, a small child cried out in terror, and others began to cry. There was a panicked feel to the tempo and the ferocity of the next assault as the bare fist of a woman with tears in her eyes hammered desperately against the door before turning to run. The two staff members who were in the hallway glanced at each other uncertainly. A shattering silence now filled the void left by the explosion of noise that had so rudely jolted them into a state of anxiety. Their eyes shared an understanding that something was amiss. It was not yet light, and they had been working since the previous evening to ensure that the younger and more vulnerable orphans had someone available to comfort them when they experienced night terrors or suffered bed-wetting incidents.

Normally, people used the knocker when bringing donations, gifts, and lost children. Usually, they announced their presence with a light, rhythmic tap, not a violent pounding. Something was wrong. Miriam, who was nearest to the door and the most practical of the two, abruptly looked away from the dark eyes of her colleague, breaking the brief spell that had locked their eyes in mutual foreboding. She had worked at the orphanage for over fifteen years and knew its rhythms, sounds, and smells intimately. Shaking off the last tendrils of shock and alarm that the unexpected and violent pounding had cast up on her, Miriam moved towards the door and pensively lifted the bar. She was surprised to see that there was no one there as she looked left and right, yet there was nobody to be seen.

The orphanage was in a poor part of Nazareth, and the streets were narrow and maze-like. It would not take a person more than a few seconds to disappear in the myriad of small streets and alleyways from the doorway of the orphanage. It was probably just kids messing around, she thought. Sometimes, other children liked to taunt the motherless children who lived in the building.

Looking up, she could still see that strange star that had been present in the far distance, and she noticed that it had stopped moving and had settled in the sky to the South, having moved from the East over several weeks. It made her feel uneasy; just like the sudden banging on the door, it was out of place. It was bizarre. It didn't move around the night sky in concert with all the other constellations, and she thought it was a bad omen.

Miriam was shaken from her thoughts by her colleague Leah. "Look, there is a parcel on the floor," she whispered, clearly still unnerved. Her weathered face still held signs of tension as she pointed a bony finger at the parcel on the step. It was bound in rough cloth and tied with coarse string. There was lots of string; in fact, the package was almost completely bound with the harsh cordage, and there was something creepy about the shape. She pushed her doubts aside and tried to ignore the warning signals that her instincts whispered urgently to her pounding heart. She squatted down to pick up the package. It was soft and heavy as she moved her hands under it. As she was trying to comprehend what it may contain, she suddenly let out a piercing scream and moved. Miriam recoiled violently, fell backwards, and banged her head into the heavy door. Her large maternal eyes flared wide with surprise before screwing themselves shut as she winced in pain as Leah swore in the background. She was middle-aged and slightly overweight, which made a dignified return to the standing position more difficult than it would have been for a younger person.

"Oh shit, it's a baby!" she said, with her hand over her mouth. "Quick, Leah, get the Director." Leah turned on the spot, her frizzy grey hair bouncing slightly as she walked swiftly away to find the man who was nicknamed the "Orphan Keeper" by the wider community, much to his dislike.

Miriam snatched up the parcel and took it straight into the kitchen, intent on cutting the twine before the infant sustained an injury or suffocated. Laying the bundle on the table, she gently started to cut at the string nearest to where the baby's neck was, taking care to ensure the blade was cutting away from the screaming and writhing package. It didn't sound human, and the screams were animal-like; a guttural roar accompanied the baby's head being released from its bonds. The Director entered the room; a look of shock etched on his face as he took in the disturbing scene of Miriam sawing at the last strands of twine that bound the baby. He was a tall, angular man with a hooked nose and protruding eyes, a feature which was exacerbated by his reaction to the ungodly scene unfolding on the kitchen table in front of him.

Leah followed him, describing in rushed tones how the baby had been discovered, and entered just in time to witness Miriam lifting the baby into her arms in an attempt to calm it. The child, now freed from its horrendous delivery sack, began to calm down. He was clearly a newborn with a very recently cut umbilical cord, and yet as he relaxed and his features became calm, his all-knowing eyes unnerved all who looked into them. His skin looked waxy and sallow. He was pale and had a slightly unnatural look that Miriam could not quite pin down.

"I have never, in all my time here, witnessed such a horrendous delivery of a child," said the Director as he ran his hand through his thinning hair before shaking his head. "Why would someone do that?" He asked no one in particular.

"Leah, find some linen to wrap him in. Miriam, please could you check him over to ensure he has no wounds or maladies," he added.

"Of course," replied Miriam as Leah nodded and hurried off to complete her new task.

Miriam's examination of the boy resulted in a fresh wave of crying and screaming as she gently prodded and poked potentially sore areas with her firm but maternal hands. Despite her efforts, the baby seemed to grow more and more distraught, and she was sure she saw fleeting moments of pure hate and aggression in the infant's eyes. *It must be the bang on the head,* she told herself. Her head was beginning to throb from a combination of her earlier collision with the door and the baby's manic screams.

Leah entered the room with swaddling cloths, bringing Miriam a welcome distraction, and soon, the little one was wrapped up snugly. Still, the crying would not stop.

"He is hungry," said Leah, matter-of-factly. "I will get some milk from the goats."

As Leah left, Miriam used her little finger to try to soothe the baby boy while she waited for Leah to return. As she popped it into the baby's mouth, her eyes once again widened in shock. She could feel sharp little teeth emerging through the gums at the front corners of his mouth. She gasped in surprise. The earliest that she had ever witnessed this was at four months old, and most did not start teething until six months of age. She turned her hand over to feel the bottom gum and was astounded to find the same there.

"What?" asked the Director as he read Miriam's incredulous expression.

"He has got teeth," whispered Miriam uncertainly.

"Impossible, he is only a couple of days old."

"Aghhh!" Screamed Miriam as the baby bit hard into the fleshy tip of her little finger. "Little bastard!" She cursed loudly, trying desperately to retrieve her finger without hurting the baby.

"Remember where you are," the Director said in calm, hushed tones before continuing, "They might all be little bastards in here, but it is not good to remind them of the fact." His look was gently chastising.

As Miriam worked her finger out of the baby's mouth, its demeanour had changed significantly. Its eyes focused on her, and the little boy gave a little giggle.

"I'm bleeding," she observed as she looked into the eerie blue eyes of the latest addition to the orphanage.

They named him Jacob, a child of the night, born in the same year as Jesus, yet destined to walk the earth for eternity. Not that he or anyone around him knew it yet. He was different from the other children; his eyes were cold and distant, his skin was pale, and his small, barely noticeable fangs were a subtle portent of the eternal life that coursed through his veins as the story of his arrival made its way through the local grapevine. The villagers, terrified and fascinated, whispered of his strange birth and the mystery of his origins.

Some were convinced that he was the one King Herod, the Roman puppet king, wanted to kill, as he had been told that the star over Bethlehem had heralded the birth of the new King of the Jews. As this was a direct threat to his rule, he had ordered the slaughter of all baby boys under the age of two years old in the area, inflicting untold horrors on thousands of young mothers and fathers. Had this child been brought from Bethlehem to protect him from the massacre of the innocents? Little did they know that the true target of Herod's massacre was currently safe in Egypt. His Father, Joseph, had been warned by an angel to leave Judea to save his son from the murderous intentions of Herod's soldiers.

As he grew, Jacob was a sickly and weak child and was often the target of the more malicious souls he shared the orphanage with. One of the worst of these vile creatures was Paulus. He was big for his age and slightly chubby. His eyes contained a hardness and arrogance that had been honed by his past. Jacob placed the dolls in between the covers on the straw mattress that served as his bed. Straw was easy to replace and burned easily, which helped the staff to maintain some level of hygiene. He hid them from casual view, ensuring that no prying eyes could see his precious creations as he tucked them away lovingly, as he wondered what it would actually be like to live with a real family. *Most children do, why can't I?* He mused as he headed back to the courtyard to join in with the others. He just wanted to play and have some fun, to dispel the sad feelings that the dolls had unexpectedly stirred in him.

As he made his way back to the courtyard, he approached the doorway, already imagining joining the game with the other children. A small smile formed at the corners of his mouth. The doorway was suddenly blocked by Paulus' menacing bulk. "Where are you going, you little viper?" he asked, a cruel half-smile on his lips and his hard, emotionless eyes fixed on Jacob. "Are you coming through here?"

Jacob stood about ten feet away and nodded uncertainly. His smile was dead on his face before it could form fully. It always started like this. The banal questions that would inevitably lead to a beating as Paulus toyed with his prey. Jacob had seen him do it more times than he could remember. He shuffled forward cautiously, not sure of how to proceed and, at the same time, knowing the outcome would be the same regardless of what he did or how he acted. Paulus slid to the side like the lizard he was, allowing Jacob access to the door. "RUN!" he bawled. Jacob's taut nerves sent a shock through his body, and he darted forward in a bid to get past Paulus and into the courtyard, where he could dodge and weave until Paulus got bored and found another victim. As he approached the opening, he felt a sense of elation, and he was going to make it! His sense of victory was rudely snatched from him as he felt Paulus kick his legs from underneath him. In the split second that he fell, he knew it was going to hurt. Abruptly, his bare knees hit the hard stone floor, causing a flash of pain, and he desperately tried to avoid injuring his face by putting his hands out. Pain shot through his wrist as it fractured under the skin, and he let out such an anguished and unnatural cry of pain that all the other orphans froze and turned towards the source of it.

"A little viper slithering on his belly," Paulus yelled towards the stunned children, who stared back in varying degrees of terror and angry resignation. None of them saw what happened, but all could guess; they were just glad it was not them this time. The agony in Jacob's wrist was so excruciating that it robbed all other thoughts from his young and vulnerable mind. He was vaguely aware of the insults rained down on him by Paulus and could not distinguish when they had stopped and were replaced by the concerned voices of staff tending to him and the harsher ones trying to chase the other children away to preserve what little dignity he had left. As they gently lifted him to his feet, Jacob came eye to eye with one of the younger orphans who was trying to crawl between the legs of one of the staff with a look of ghoulish delight on his face. He was happy to have witnessed a little bit of drama in his otherwise drab and hopeless little life.

An hour later, after Jacob had been bandaged up by Miriam, Leah led him gently to his sleeping mat, crooning and urging him to rest. She left him there to undress and wished him a good night.

"Night, Ma'am," he replied, his boyish voice high and wavering. He sniffed again, trying to hold the tears at bay, and tried to cheer himself up by pretending he was going home to his parents, the ones he had made earlier. *It will be alright one day;* he mused as he reflected on the pride he felt in making dolls earlier and pulled back his blanket. What he saw overwhelmed his tender grasp on his self-control, and it slipped away, replaced with gasping sobs of deep sorrow and despair. The bastard Paulus had snapped the heads, arms, and legs off both dolls and rearranged the parts in a macabre tableau. When his tears stopped and he was able to look closer, he was disturbed to find that Paulus had even scratched out their eyes. *They will never see me again.* His child's mind screamed inside his head, and he sobbed softly as he crawled under the blanket, alone with a broken heart and his wrist throbbing painfully.

The strange little craving came and went as he slept fitfully, disturbed by the nocturnal movements, snores, and occasional cries of the other orphans. He dreamed of sheep and goats; he was a herder, and he was free to roam the hills, where he found happiness. In his dream, he had sat down under an olive tree to escape the heat of the midday sun, when suddenly his blood ran cold. In the corner of his eye, he noticed a wolf slipping out of a dense patch of bushes. It moved slowly; its belly low to the ground. He knew that wolves mostly attacked at night and hid out in secure areas during the day. Strange. Then another wolf stealthily emerged from the thicket; Jacob realised he had brought his flock to the wolf's lair and had literally brought lambs to the slaughter. In a split second, the pair of wolves, having got close enough to their prey, attacked viciously, bringing the lamb to the ground and scattering the rest of the flock.

In a rage, Jacob sprinted over to the nearest wolf with an ungodly scream emanating from his lips. A feeling of immense power ran through him, and like an unexpected lightning bolt from the sky, Jacob leapt onto the wolf's back and bit deeply into the animal's neck, instinctively finding the jugular vein. The wolf made a strange keening noise as its partner backed off slowly, its eyes locked on Jacob's. The eyes of the wolf were both predatory and knowing, and Jacob sensed an uneasy kinship between himself and the animal. The blood refreshed him and made him feel more alive than he had ever felt in his life, and he revelled in his newfound power. Suddenly, he was jolted from his sleep by the staff shouting the wake-up call. His newfound strength withered only to be replaced with the pain in his arm and a desperate thirst that he just couldn't slake.

Jacob grew up quickly, his appetite growing with him. He was different from the other children; his eyes were cold and distant, his skin was pale, and his strength was uncanny. He fed on the village animals at first, his thirst for blood unquenchable, but as he matured, he longed for the taste of human blood. To avoid the constant persecution dished out by Paulus, he would spend as much time as possible away from the orphanage. The beatings had become weekly occurrences, and the threats and verbal abuse left Jacob feeling small and degraded. At times, it robbed him of his ability to hope for a better life and weakened his confidence, leaving him feeling that he would never succeed at anything. He would lurk in the shadows, watching the villagers go about their lives, feeling a deep loneliness amidst the bustling town.

One night, he couldn't resist the temptation any longer. He bit into the neck of an elderly passing villager, drinking deeply of his life force. Soon, word spread of the monster among them, and the villagers, in fear for their lives, banded together to hunt him down. Jacob, sensing their intentions, hid in the darkness of the orphanage whilst the people searched for the killer, sure the perpetrator was an adult. He was ashamed of his own actions, disgusted by what he had done, yet strengthened by it undeniably. He had to find a way to gain blood without drawing the suspicion of the authorities and the deadly consequences that they could bring to him.

Jacob's life had been one of struggle and hardship until he discovered the restorative and energising power of blood. His strength grew as he surreptitiously fed on animals and the odd fresh corpse he could find in the dark streets of the poorer areas of the town. He would sneak out at night and hunt for a source of blood, feeling himself grow stronger with every taste of it. The blood of dead humans, he noticed, tasted stale, and although they helped him to grow, they were nowhere near as rich in life-giving properties as the blood of the living. It depressed him that to live, he would have to kill. But having been an orphan in a poor and brutal orphanage, he had had to fight for survival every day. He would find a way. His pale and weak appearance, combined with his small and weak body, had made him an easy target for bullies, and he often found both solace and regret in his dark thoughts. However, now he had one thing that kept him going and gave him hope: his thirst for blood. Although he didn't know he needed it at first. It had been a strange and violent type of hunger that left him confused. It was there but unfulfilled. He didn't understand his craving or his need for it, but now he knew that not having it made him a ghost of a human being.

After his first kill, his pale pallor had faded, and he had grown in both stature and confidence. He continued to feed and expand his access to the recently departed on crucifixes, mortuaries, and streets. He was careful to avoid the diseased and only drank from the executed and accident-prone. He was careful to find veins and arteries normally covered by clothing and avoided the neck at all costs. The femoral artery was his favourite place, and he would make a small incision to create a tiny flap of skin under which he could insert a thin needle to pierce the artery. He would then suck the blood from the hole.

The window for harvesting blood from fresh corpses was quite narrow. Beyond four hours, it was reasonable. Over eight, it was sort of okay, but Jacob considered anything over sixteen hours to be emergency rations. Once he had drunk his fill, he would ensure that no traces of blood remained at the site of the wound and would press the flap of skin back in place, secure in the knowledge that the incision would not bleed as the heart had stopped hours ago and the blood was beginning to pool in the lower parts of the body.

Despite his physical growth and the continued development of his macabre skills, Jacob felt he had not reached his zenith, and he decided to wait until he had the overwhelming and superior power he would need, not just to best his enemy but to launch himself forward into the world on his own terms. Over the next six months, he grew and seemed to develop a wolflike quality. Whether this was due to his covert nightly activities or his regular diet of human and animal blood, it was impossible to say.

Still, like a relentless tide, Paulus' persecution washed over the orphanage, pulling under anyone who dared to resist the force of his beatings and intimidation. Each day brought new torments, each calculated to erode the children's spirits and break their resilience. Whispers of defiance were swiftly extinguished with harsh punishments, and even the smallest act of kindness became a dangerous rebellion. A heavy atmosphere of fear permeated the halls, silencing laughter and replacing it with the constant dread of Paulus' next cruelty.

CHAPTER II

When Jacob could, he left the orphanage and wandered the streets, markets, and bazaars. During these explorations, he felt at peace away from the ever noisy and oppressive orphanage. Several years ago, he met an enigmatic figure who would ultimately burn fast and bright before being brutally extinguished. He would cast a shadow that would create hope and despair for thousands of years. The boy had an extraordinary calmness that far surpassed his years. As it later turned out, it was he who had been Herod's target, not Jacob, despite what the spiteful Nazareth gossips said. Yeshua was affectionately known to many as Josh. As a child, he stood apart from his peers, possessing a profound sense of peace and a deep intelligence that left those around him both intrigued and puzzled. His charisma was unmatched, and his reputation was peppered with claims of unique powers that he often wielded to escape chores or sidestep the mundane trials of childhood. Always spouting bizarre philosophies, Jacob was drawn to him, and they became good friends.

There had been rumours that Josh had not always been so peaceful. There were stories of him killing children in the village when he was as young as five years old. Jacob had heard that on one sabbath day, Josh had been frolicking in a stream, making little pools and sparrows out of clay. An adult had supposedly reprimanded him for working on the Sabbath, at which point Josh told his clay birds to go away. They immediately became flesh and blood and flew away, much to the surprise of those present. At this point, the young boy with the adult who had admonished Josh began to demolish the pools with a stick before Josh cursed him, causing the child to wither up and die. The legend suggested that Josh was shocked and surprised by his own powers and quickly ran off home. On his way, another boy who collided with the young Josh also died instantly, as panicked Josh cursed him too. The townsfolk, scared for the safety of their children, soon gathered and petitioned Josh's Dad to control his son. According to the rumours, Josh became angry at the fact that certain villagers had snitched on him, so he cursed the petitioners, who all became blind.

Still, there were more fantastic stories of him raising another boy from the dead. The myth told of a boy who had been playing on a roof and had fallen to his death, and all the kids who were there quickly scattered, running to their local homes in an impossible attempt to disassociate themselves from the tragic event. Josh remained calm and stayed with the dead boy, but when his parents arrived, they instantly accused Josh of pushing the stricken boy to his death. This was most likely based on his previous reputation, which was caused by the earlier rumours. Josh was incensed by this accusation and resurrected the boy who corroborated Josh's version of events, much to the joy and fear of his tearful parents. Still, Jacob did not know Josh then, and life in the orphanage taught him not to rely on the hearsay and gossip that was often brought to life by dark motives. All of this combined to lend Josh a sort of street credibility and mystery that further drew Jacob to him.

As Josh grew, so did the mythology that surrounded him. Those who witnessed his gentle nature and heard his radical ideas could not even begin to imagine the transformative path on which he would embark. Small wonder then that, although he appeared as just another unusual kid with eccentric musings, Josh would evolve into one of the most significant figures in human history. Jacob had no idea that he would spend the next 2000 years dealing with the consequences of Josh's short existence and its conflicting human interpretations. He remained sceptical and would not be impressed with any of the versions of the beliefs that followed Judaism. They all say, "Thou shalt not kill," and yet, generation after generation would engage in pointless, futile wars. Scenes of thousands of battles and disasters would flash through his mind in the future as he pondered the events of his extraordinarily long life.

Josh was not merely a child; he had the makings of a revered teacher, a visionary healer, and an unwavering friend. Jacob dismissed his influence as eccentric at first, but it later revealed a deeper resonance that stretched across time and cultures. He was more than just an innovative thinker; perhaps he bore a divine spark. The echoes of his philosophies would leave an indelible mark on Jacob as his life stretched across the long centuries. It would fuel future conflicts, ignite scientific debates, and challenge established norms.

Unaware of his own immortality, Jacob had no idea of what the future would hold for him. He could not know that when the Romans got bored of feeding Christians to the lions, nailing them to crosses and turning them into human candles, they would create the Roman Catholic Church and delete all the fun stuff. Josh would not have wanted it that way, but he didn't live long enough to do anything about it, and his words undid him. Never show your hand and always keep a straight face was Jacob's mantra. It was a survival mechanism honed from an early age in the mean orphanage that was the backdrop to his existence.

When the Roman Empire eventually started to fail, they began to lose control. That was when they would decide that their polytheistic religion, which allowed people to make their own choices and find their own moral compass, should be replaced with a monotheistic one that would dictate it. Their approach was inspired by the fact that they could no longer police the citizens of their great empire, so God and the Devil would have to instead.

The omnipresent watchful eye of the one all-powerful god deciding on a citizen's afterlife would keep people in check, whilst the Devil stoked the flames of Hell, eager for the souls of wrongdoers. It would be a carrot and a stick on a biblical scale. When Emperor Constantine eventually converted to Christianity in 312 AD, he ensured that Christianity became the official faith of the mighty Roman Empire, and it was inevitable that it would face resistance. People would not like having just one God who said you were born bad, so you better make up for it. To overcome this, the Romans would simply Christianise the old ways. Josh was not born in December of the year zero. He was born in March, around 6 BC. How could King Herod target him in year zero when he died in 4 BC? Jacob always found this fact hilarious, but also wondered if it was he or Josh that Herod had sent his brutally efficient soldiers to target.

It steeled him to the lies and brutality of future governments and regimes not yet conceived when Jacob would look back over his extraordinarily long life in over two thousand years' time. Herod's slaughter of the innocents reminded him of the cold-eyed Nazi SS Soldiers who hung that little boy in Auschwitz. One boy and three men were executed together. The men died fast, their body weight snapping their necks in an efficient application of German engineering, physics, and indoctrination. The boy took his time, though. His little body convulsed and twisted for a full three minutes, losing control of his bladder and bowels as the inmates looked on, helpless to intervene. Anger, disbelief, and resignation stood amongst the people in the gathered crowd, and they were personified by the expressions horrendously etched in the expressions of the inmates. There were two suicides later that day, and six other inmates were shot for arbitrary offences.

"Where is god?" muttered a dejected and emaciated inmate, who had previously run a successful watch-making business.

"There is no God. If there were, he would not let this happen." Said the man next to him as a tear ran down silently from his eye."

"God is dead," he whispered.

Those were tough days. Even though Jacob would experience the horrors of war as applied by Genghis Khan and hundreds of other psychopaths, this day would always stand out in his memory. I'm a killer, too; just move on. It's just death, and everyone dies! Apart from me came the bitter afterthought.

Jacob had once said to Josh, "The road to hell is paved with good intentions," in response to one of Josh's philosophical musings. It later became a standard phrase, and no one knew it was first uttered two thousand years ago by an immortal vampire in jest.

Yet, the irony of Josh's tragic fate would linger. The day he was taken would become a stark reminder to future generations of the perilous path that accompanies those who dare to challenge the prevailing order. It would echo throughout history. Even in his death, the indomitable nature of his influence would be palpable. In the not-so-distant future, Jacob would witness the death of his childhood friend as a soldier and would realise later that he had also witnessed the end of an era. A tear would slip quietly from behind his helmet. He would always remember Josh's unwavering spirit, which would continue to inspire and enrage future generations. Silly bastard got yourself killed, he would think regretfully at the time. His military discipline forced him to watch impassively as the nails were crudely driven through Josh's arms and feet. His screams sang a song of pain that accompanied the inexorable rhythm of the hammer blows.

However, history is a tricky fabric woven with threads of truth and layers of distortion. The narrative of Josh's life would be twisted and reshaped by the hands of the Romans and countless theologians, often straying from the essence of his original message. Yet, as an invisible observer and one who had witnessed the unfolding of countless cataclysmic events, the truth remained intact. It was not just etched in documents but ingrained in Jacob's memory.

Reflecting on Josh's life two thousand years later brought to mind the poignant words of John Lennon, who once provocatively claimed that the Beatles were more popular than Christ. This comparison was met with scorn. Jacob agreed: Josh mania, no TV, but ranting mobs. Beatle mania: TV and mobs. Crazy sheeple. Back then, in Josh's time, the avenues for spreading ideas were far less sophisticated. In contrast, Josh's teachings, at once revolutionary and subversive, cut through the fabric of society, challenging the very foundations of belief and setting nations against each other in deadly conflicts.

Throughout the shadows of history, where both light and dark would take firm and opposing stances. Jacob was to witness atrocities that would have been unimaginable to the average mind at the time of his birth. He would learn the harsh lesson that the world is filled with predators lurking just out of sight and sometimes right in front of you, disguised with a cloak of innocence. He was a natural protector born of desperation and conflict; he sought to defend the vulnerable, embodied by his commitment to justice, and would never bow to passive acceptance. The proverbial "eye for an eye" might have incited dissent and gone against Josh's "turn the other cheek" idea, but that never sat right with Jacob. In his younger days, he just hungered to live, and he did what he had to do to survive. Thoughts of the future were limited to escaping the orphanage and the clutches of the monster that was Paulus.

CHAPTER III

Despite Paulus' constant torment, Jacob never gave up. He knew that his thirst for blood, once satisfied, would make him strong enough to stand up to this bully eventually. He longed for the day when he would no longer be the victim but the victor. Blood had become his source of power, and he would not rest until he had his fill. He was still growing and learning. Every time Paulus attacked him, Jacob could feel his strength increasing, and he used the attacks as opportunities to study the cruel methods of his nemesis; he would then devise ways of countering Paulus' aggression. Slowly, a plan began to form in his mind. It was only partial, but it was beginning to take shape. He could sense the growing power coursing through his veins, giving him the courage to fight back. He had always been small and weak, but now things were changing, and he could feel himself growing stronger with each passing day. He knew that it was all because of his unquenchable thirst for blood and his ability to source it.

The other orphans noticed the changes in him, too, and over the next few months, they became as afraid of Jacob as they were of Paulus. There was no reason for their fear as they watched the continuing victimisation of Jacob by Paulus, and Jacob never threatened any of the other children. If anything, he was positively helpful towards them. The fear was deeper than that, and it was instinctual.

Something had changed in him; something animalistic had replaced the scared little boy, and he had developed the aura of a cobra waiting to strike. Jacob had started to see hints of fear in the bully's eyes as he started to resist him for the first time, testing his strength without displaying it fully. Soon, he would no longer be Paulus' punching bag. Jacob knew that he had finally reached a turning point. He was no longer the weak and defenceless orphan but a force to be reckoned with. It would soon be time to apply that force.

After his last beating, Jacob waited until the others were sleeping and left the orphanage, the bruising on his ribs and face a throbbing reminder of his victimhood. As he vanished into the darkness, a sense of purpose overtook him. He no longer had to choose between being a sheep or a wolf; he could be both. A wolf that protected the innocent and a sheep that fought back against the ever-present cruelty in the world. No longer did he have to hide in the shadows. He could use them to his advantage. With each step he took, he knew he could have left a trail of destruction in his wake. A necessary destruction, one that would ensure the safety of those who were vulnerable. He couldn't help but wonder if his actions would be remembered in a positive light or if he would forever be seen as a ruthless killer. In the end, it didn't matter to him. As long as he made a difference in the world, that was all that mattered. He had found his purpose and his true identity, and even though it sickened him somewhat, he could not deny it. No longer would he be confined by society's labels; he was his own person. He wanted to be the wolf that protected the sheep in the orphanage. His mind's eye flashed back to Paulus viciously punching him to the ground and mercilessly kicking his ribs in. As he took a deep breath, he felt the echoes of that beating. Jacob needed one more good feed, and then he would be ready. He had gauged Paulus' weaknesses and could sense that Paulus feared a potential challenge to his status. It was probably why there had been an increase in the frequency and severity of the beatings. They were an attempt to maintain dominance. Jacob was careful to appear weak. There was no point in warning Paulus what was coming; it was best to play the part of a meek little lamb.

He knew he would have to be careful in his selection of targets. They couldn't just be any criminals; they had to be the worst of the bunch. The ones who preyed on the weak and vulnerable, taking advantage of those who couldn't defend themselves. He had already gathered a list of potential victims and was searching for those with visible signs of corruption and greed. He would be their reckoning, the one who would bring them to justice for their crimes. For every innocent victim they had harmed, he would make sure they paid in full, with their lives and with their blood. He was the wolf that protected the sheep, and he would stop at nothing to rid the world of these parasites. They may have thought they were above the law, but he would make sure that they would end up below the earth. They would face the consequences of their actions. He was a vigilante in a lawless place. He prowled the night without success and returned to the orphanage unsatisfied, and fell into a troubled slumber, frustrated by his inability to find a suitable target.

CHAPTER IV

Josh was always bitterly complaining about the moneylenders who shamelessly used the sacred temples to peddle their financial services to the desperate. They would lure in the vulnerable with promises of quick cash, only to charge exorbitant interest rates that left them trapped in a cycle of crushing debt, some even selling themselves into slavery.

These predators preyed on the most impoverished, using brutal tactics to strip them of whatever little they had. They left behind a trail of broken souls. The stench of their greed and exploitation permeated every corner of the town, suffocating those who dared to dream of a better life. Josh, with fire in his eyes and a quiver in his voice, would often recount the horror stories of those who fell victim to these merciless loan sharks. His words were like a haunting melody, evoking anger, fear, and pity. He was a complex character with a deep sense of justice and a burning desire to right the wrongs of a corrupt system.

As he spoke, the scent of incense and the sound of temple bells seemed to fade into the background, replaced by the cries of the oppressed and the echoes of their struggles. These people preyed on the poorest and most desperate, using gangster methods to deprive the vulnerable of their few possessions, leaving them destitute and often beaten their bruises left as receipts of their debt.

Towards the end of the day, one of these low-life scumbags carelessly ploughed into Jacob, sending him reeling. But that wasn't enough for the vile creature. He had to add insult to injury, unleashing a barrage of verbal abuse and then striking Jacob in the face, drawing blood from his tender upper lip. Jacob had always prided himself on his self-control and his ability to resist the alluring call of human blood. But as he stood there, reeling from the shock of the attack and tasting his own blood, something inside him snapped. He felt a primal hunger take hold of him, a hunger that had been suppressed for far too long. In that moment, he made a solemn promise to himself, fuelled by a deep, undying commitment.

"I will have your blood on my lips before the week is through," he growled, his voice dripping with malice.

He felt a surge of power as he vocalised the threat, his eyes boring into the back of the arrogant moneylender, who continued on his way as if nothing had happened. Your fate is now sealed, Jacob thought.

He stalked the moneylender to his lavish estate, moving silently through the deepening shadows until he found a concealed spot from which to observe. He waited for hours, his muscles tensed and ready for action. As night descended, he surveyed the perimeter with a steely gaze. Finally, he deemed it safe to make his move, but just as he was about to set foot on the property, his plans were thwarted by the sudden arrival of two seductive-looking women. He watched in frustration as they entered the house, their flirtatious laughter echoing in the night. His blood boiled with a mixture of anger and desire. They were like sirens, drawing him deeper into their web, yet he couldn't afford to lose sight of his primary target, the arsehole money-lender. With a heavy heart, he tore himself away from the alluring distraction and refocused on his mission.

He would have to find another way in; he knew his determination and cunning would see him through. For now, he bided his time, waiting for the perfect moment to strike. The stakes were high, and he was willing to do whatever it took to ensure his success. The darkness provided the perfect cover for his calculated and deadly scheme. The intensity surrounding his mission only grew, and for a moment, he considered killing all three.

After what seemed like hours, the ladies left, their drunken goodbyes hanging in the cold night air. This was it; this was his chance. He resolved himself to wait another hour. When he struck, he struck hard and mercilessly.

The moneylender who had rudely collided with him earlier didn't stand a chance. He was half-drunk and did not expect to receive any more company that night, let alone fight for his life. Jacob was more than just a vampire; he was a force to be reckoned with if you fell foul of him. As he advanced towards his prey, his senses heightened, taking in every detail of the scene: the smell of fear emanating from the moneylender, the sound of his victim's laboured breathing, the sight of his own shadow moving in the moonlight.

"Remember me?" Jacob asked casually.

"No, who are you, and what do you want?" snapped the moneylender.

"You bumped into me earlier."

"I bump into a lot of people, so what?"

Jacob did not reply and closed the distance between them in a split second. Driven by adrenaline, rage, and bloodlust, he sank his fangs into the arrogant bastard's neck and drove him savagely onto the hard stone floor. He drank freely and deeply; the fresh blood brought an almost instant change. As the moneylender's life ebbed away, Jacob's life force seemed to grow. He felt stronger than ever before, and a sense of invincibility descended on him, soothing the savage emotions that had held him tight in their grip only a few moments ago. He felt a fundamental tear deep inside of him, as if his true self had finally been born. The realisation of this fact was liberating. He knew that he would never go back to his old life as the same person. He was now a true predator, and he would relish every moment of it.

CHAPTER V

He had drained the life from the moneylender's jugular, taking the man's very essence, just as the man himself had bled the destitute people of the area he had always known. The cobbled streets, the Roman aqueducts, and their rule of law had earned the respect and the hatred of the local populace in equal measure. Jacob thought he had gained strength before, but this latest draught made him feel practically undefeatable. A new confidence was growing, and the world seemed less frightening.

His mind swam as he walked back toward the orphanage, intent on delivering an overdue justice to Paulus. Am I ready, though? he thought, but immediately knew a quick death for Paulus would be far too kind. The power he wielded, and the control over his own destiny it afforded him, felt liberating. He had never felt more alive. The rush of adrenaline, the taste of blood, the sense of invincibility, it was all he had ever truly wanted, along with freedom. He had always been an outcast, a forgotten orphan in a world ruled by the strong and vindictive. Now, he was the hunter, not the hunted, and he vowed that no one would ever prey on him again. His thoughts focused unblinkingly on Paulus and what he would do.

Paulus deserved to suffer, just as he had made others suffer, and Jacob, the wolf, would be the one to deliver that justice. He was ready for this new life, this new potential. He imagined himself in the dark, standing by Paulus' bed, staring down. He felt anger and hatred coursing through his veins. He had been wronged by this repulsive young man, and now it was his turn to seek revenge. He couldn't help but envision the satisfaction of sinking his fangs into Paulus' neck, watching the life drain from his eyes. It was almost poetic justice. This wasn't just about revenge; it was a necessary change and rebirth, a rite of passage. He had spent his entire existence being looked down upon, treated as nothing, and told to be thankful for it.

Now, with his newfound abilities, Jacob could shape his reality. He would use this power to rise above his oppressors, to show them he was no longer weak. He was ready to embrace his true potential and leave behind the injustices he had faced. He was determined to forge his own path and leave behind the shackles of his past. He would no longer be defined by his mysterious origins, but by his strength, his resilience, and his unwavering will. As he prepared to face Paulus, he knew change was coming but couldn't fully imagine the shape it would take. His thoughts were interrupted as he reached the orphanage and began the tricky combination of climbs required to bypass the gate and reach the exterior steps leading into the dormitory. Getting caught outside after bedtime meant a beating from the staff, yet he felt strangely unafraid. The absence of fear was a new sensation, and Jacob liked it. He made his way quietly up to the dormitory, his footsteps solid and sure. He knew exactly what he was going to do. A wicked smile danced across his face, partially hidden in the shadows.

As he crept over to Paulus' prostrate figure, he knew he had the element of surprise in the dark hours. He felt a sense of satisfaction. He had been pushed around and beaten by Paulus for far too long, and now he was in control. With the oil from the lamp, he began Paulus' decline. He had decided Paulus' undoing would be slow, torturous, and humiliating. He wanted to repay what Paulus had done to him, wanting him to feel the fear and helplessness Jacob had endured. He took his time, pouring drops of oil on Paulus' chest and watching it soak in. He applied a little more, knowing the blanket would act as a wick and sustain the fire without the flames spreading out of control. Paulus snored softly, completely unaware of the judgment about to be visited upon him. Jacob used the flame from the lamp to ignite the blanket and, as the fire took hold, he bent close.

"Wake up, darling, you're on fire," he whispered into Paulus' ear, the tone sickeningly gentle, like a mother to a child.

He did this because he wanted to maximise the cruelty of being an orphan alongside the fear of death that all mortals feel.

Quickly, Jacob's strong hand pressed down

hard on Paulus' mouth, leaving the nostrils open to smell the burning threat of his destruction. Paulus' eyes were wide with panic, physically unable to fight back. His face received a vicious slap followed by the shock of cold piss thrown from a chamber pot, which extinguished the flames.

"I won't wake you up next time," crooned Jacob, giving him a gentle smile. It would have been easier just to kill him, but Jacob had other plans. "An eye for an eye, a tooth for a tooth." Josh was always banging on about that sort of stuff and then saying things like 'turn the other cheek' and 'blessed are the peacemakers.' It made no sense; it was contradictory. Jacob had just realised the truth of survival. It was about the survival of the strong, or evolution, as it would become known in the future. The strong survive, and without a protector, the weak die.

CHAPTER VI

The next morning, Paulus stumbled into the canteen, his once proud stance now replaced with a slumped posture. He could feel the weight of the previous night's shameful events pressing heavily on his shoulders. Rumours of his bed-wetting habits had spread like wildfire, leaving him feeling exposed and vulnerable. It wasn't even his own piss. As he made his way through the crowded room, he could sense the whispers and sniggers that followed him like a dark cloud. It wasn't just the humiliation that haunted Paulus; there was something else lurking in the shadows, something more sinister and menacing: Jacob. The mere thought of him sent shivers down Paulus' spine. Since that night, he felt he could never escape the watchful gaze of that calculating, cold-eyed boy. How did he get so strong? Paulus asked himself. Even when Jacob wasn't directly in his line of sight, Paulus could feel his presence, like a dark spectre looming over him. Throughout the day, Paulus tried to keep his head down and avoid any further humiliation. Something had changed in Jacob; an animalistic shift Paulus could not quite place. He felt a sense of danger emanating from Jacob whenever he came near or when those cold eyes fixed on him with that predatory caress.

When a young orphan boy mocked him, something inside Paulus snapped. Without a second thought, he lashed out and beat the boy, fuelled by a mix of anger and embarrassment. As he stood there, panting and sweating, he could feel Jacob's cold eyes boring into him, silently judging his every move. Later, when Jacob approached him, Paulus' heart raced in fear. But instead of a reprimand, Jacob simply tutted and mimed ticking off a note on a piece of paper. It was then that Paulus began to feel the true extent of Jacob's control.

Each week, they would exchange bedding, and the returned linen would be ticked off the original issue list, nothing sinister, but now it seemed that Jacob was keeping a tally of Paulus' indiscretions. As the day went on, Paulus couldn't shake the feeling of being watched and judged. He knew that Jacob had noted at least three of his mistakes where he had treated other children cruelly or violently, and he couldn't help but wonder what the consequences might be. I will give him a good beating and show him who the boss is! Paulus told himself in an ineffective attempt to regain his confidence and reassert his dominance, even if only in his own mind. In his heart, he wasn't convinced, though.

As Paulus slowly undressed for bed in the dimly lit dorm room, he could feel Jacob's piercing gaze on him again. His skin prickled with unease as he glanced around. There was no mistaking it: Jacob's dark eyes were fixed on him with a sinister intensity. Paulus couldn't help but feel a shiver run down his spine as he met Jacob's unwavering gaze. The way his lips curled into a lazy smile, like a cat toying with a mouse, only added to the unsettling, acidic feeling in the pit of Paulus' stomach.

Jacob held up three fingers and spoke in a low, menacing voice. "You owe me three," he said, his eyes never leaving Paulus' face.

"Sweet dreams, darling," he added with a sly smirk, before silently pointing to his own eyes and then directly at Paulus, an unambiguous message: I'm watching you. Paulus felt a surge of fear and anger rise within him as he realised the true intentions behind Jacob's words. He could sense the malice radiating from Jacob, dark and animalistic like a predator stalking its prey. There was also a hint of something else, something shadowy and mysterious that intrigued Paulus despite his better judgement. As he lay in bed that night, Paulus couldn't shake the feeling of Jacob's eyes on his soul, haunting his every thought and driving him almost to the brink of madness. He eventually drifted off into an uneasy sleep, which was suddenly destroyed by a shocking and brutal agony as Jacob swiftly snapped his index finger.

CHAPTER VII

Jacob was astounded by what he had accomplished in such a short amount of time. He had gone from a frail and sickly child to a fierce and dominant character with the ability to take life at will. He had started to turn the tables on his oppressor, but even as he enjoyed his newfound abilities, he could feel the old weakness creeping back in. It reminded him of his past; of the years he spent being tormented and abused. Now, he was in control, and he could not let that control slip away. To maintain his newfound position in the orphanage, Jacob knew he had to kill again. The death of the moneylender had been attributed to a disgruntled customer, which worked in Jacob's favour. But he could not establish a pattern. He needed to be strategic and unpredictable. He had also noticed the hateful looks directed at him by Paulus, and was aware that they were becoming more common, bolder even. Could Paulus sense his weakening?

He decided to roam the town that night, actively searching for his next target. As he walked the dark streets, Jacob's senses were heightened. He could smell the fear of his potential victims, hear their frantic heartbeats, and see the terror in their eyes. It was exhilarating, yet also worrying. He revelled in the dominion he held over these people, and it made him feel alive as he searched for his next victim. His mind suddenly screamed: Don't victimise victims, and don't become what you hate!

As he continued his hunt, he couldn't help but feel a twinge of guilt. He was no longer the helpless orphan, yet he wanted to tear the souls from the bodies of other human beings to serve his own purposes and remain strong. He was not really comfortable with it. It was a conflicting feeling, but Jacob pushed it aside. He had to be strong to survive. The strong live, the weak die; it was demonstrated as a fact in the natural world as much as it was in the human urban environment.

As he plotted his next move, Jacob couldn't help but reflect on his transformation. He was no longer just a boy; he was a multifaceted and deadly character with complicated requirements. As much as he was empowered by it, he was also revolted by it. Yet he could not afford to lose the initiative in the orphanage. Now that his persecution of Paulus had begun, he had to maintain the momentum. He had been pushed to the brink, and now that he was pushing back, he would not let Paulus gain any advantage. He grinned and then felt a tinge of remorse. He knew he had to keep up the facade to maintain his disguise and not let others see what he had become. *What am I?* he thought uncertainly.

After a fruitless search, Jacob trudged into a dimly lit tavern, his mind clouded with frustration, confusion, and a mounting sense of anger he desperately tried to suppress. His hand was clenched tightly around a few stolen coins that he had found in the notorious moneylender's house. He hadn't been looking for money, but there had been a few coins scattered on a nearby table, close to where he had killed the man. Now I'm a thief. Bloody hell, that was a wrong turn, he thought bitterly. As he sat at the table and took a long swig of his drink, disappointment turned into anger before dissolving into sadness.

His true intention had not been to gain riches but to steal the moneylender's life and absorb his strength and vitality. Lost in his thoughts, Jacob's attention drifted to a conversation taking place behind him between two middle-aged women. Their voices were hushed, but their words were laced with intensity and intrigue. Interesting. One of them spoke of her desire to leave her husband, a man who refused to grant her a divorce. She was from a family of great wealth and social standing, while he had slowly but surely fallen from grace as his financial fortunes had ebbed away. The contrast between their fates was stark. As Jacob eavesdropped, he felt a twinge of envy. These women, with their convoluted lives, seemed to lead a far more interesting and comfortable existence than his own.

Apparently, the man in question was not violent towards his wife and had not committed adultery, but Jacob couldn't help but sense a whisper of conspiracy as he listened to the conversation unfold. They were discussing ways to get rid of the woman's husband. While Jacob knew it was none of his business, he couldn't ignore what had been said in quiet voices. Sometimes, he had to strain to pick up on the secretive details when the voices descended to a low whisper. As he casually glanced around the tavern, ensuring his eyes passed over the women without lingering, he noted the contrast between them. The one who wanted to leave her husband was plump with a pretty face, while her friend was tall and bony with sharp features. It was almost comical, and yet it only added to the inner turmoil he was feeling. They had said some truly bad things as they complained and contrived.

Jacob had always prided himself on being a good person and felt ashamed that he wasn't one anymore. Once he had matched faces to voices and had turned back to his drink, he couldn't help but wonder how he was capable of doing things that were morally wrong and yet still wanting to do good. He was already a murderer, a thief, and a bully.

The tall woman continued to talk in hushed tones about a poison maker who lived nearby.

"I will kill him," the plump woman whispered venomously.

Jacob's mind raced with thoughts of how he could stop her from going through with her plan. He heard her mention that the poison was undetectable and tasteless, and Jacob felt that a tragic plot was about to unfold. He had never considered himself a violent or vengeful person, but the thought of getting rid of someone without leaving a trace was tempting and disturbing in equal measure. He quickly dismissed such an easy death for Paulus, as he deserved worse. As the woman behind him boasted about the hundreds of doses the poisoner had sold with no one ever suspecting a thing, Jacob's mind began to race with ideas.

After another fifteen minutes of conversation, the tall woman had described the poisoner's house and location in detail. The poisoner would be his next victim; Jacob killed for strength and fed off the evil so he could protect the good. He was beginning to balance his understanding of himself, the world, and his place within it. The poisoner, on the other hand, seemed to delight in handing out liquids designed to steal the lives of innocents for whatever price the buyer chose to pay. High or low, the price did not seem to matter. Once again, he tried to question and analyse his own moral code. What moral code? He finished his drink and set off to find the poison maker's residence. From what he heard the woman say, he could work out the location easily enough. *She would have to die, he thought.* As he left the tavern, he wondered if it was safe to drink the blood of someone who had been poisoned.

CHAPTER VIII

Jacob couldn't help but feel a sense of dread. He knew deep down this was a bad idea, and yet, he couldn't seem to stop himself. He was making a choice he never thought he would make, and the weight of it sat heavily on his shoulders. As he arrived at the poison maker's doorstep and knocked loudly, Jacob couldn't shake the feeling he was making a huge mistake, but he also couldn't deny the excitement that coursed through his veins at the thought of finally gaining more strength and the prospect of another kill. It was a feeling he knew he might regret later. He pushed all negative thoughts aside and knocked on the door again, eager to get his hands on the poisoner and drain her blood so that he could complete his conquest back at the orphanage. In that moment, all that mattered was getting what he wanted, the consequences be damned. He was also aware that these were very dangerous thoughts. No answer.

His heart was pounding with anticipation and adrenaline. The three-storey building loomed before him; its dark windows and imposing structure made him feel uneasy. The living quarters were on the bottom two floors, and the windows were covered with heavy wooden shutters, but the apothecary's workshop he had heard was on the top floor caught his attention. He could feel the thrill of the hunt coursing through his veins, but was frustrated that there was no answer. He tried knocking again to no avail. He tried to find another entrance, but all the other doors seemed to lead to different properties. It seemed the poisoner's lair had only one way in and one way out.

Once again, his hunt had been stifled. He could see that there was light emanating from the top floor, but the poisoner seemed to be either sleeping or just ignoring the world. Perhaps she had the wisdom not to open the door to unexpected guests late at night. Once again, he sat and watched; time seemed to stand still in stark contrast to a desperate longing that moved and twisted within him, interrupting his thoughts and wracking his mind. The lower floor windows remained dark, and although he could not detect any discernible movement from where he sat, he felt that something sinister was brewing inside.

After an hour of waiting, he decided to take another look. He crept closer and peeked through the slats of the shutters on the lowest floor as he stretched his body to get a better view, a strange tingling sensation washed over him, unlike anything he had ever experienced before; it made him feel sick and euphoric all at once. To his amazement, he found himself rising from the ground, carried by an unseen force. He gasped in shock, but couldn't help but feel elated at the same time. The only light in the building came from the apothecary's workshop on the third floor, and as his bloodlust surged, he rose even higher. Strange, pungent smells assaulted his nostrils, and the candlelight above seemed to dance and flicker in response to his presence. What is she concocting in there? He wondered, his curiosity and excitement growing with each passing moment.

As he hovered outside the third-floor window, he couldn't help but marvel at the surprising force that had overtaken him. The conflicting emotions of fear and fascination swirled within him, and he couldn't tear his gaze away from the source of the mysterious lights and smells as he rose higher into the air. Before he reached the third floor, he risked a quick look around. He had no idea what he would do if he was spotted. As his head rose over the window ledge, he gained a view of the workshop. It was a cacophony of jars and bowls with unusual powders and liquids held within.

At the workbench, a woman stood with her back towards him, heating a bubbling liquid over an oil burner. Her posture was straight and dignified. At that moment, he understood the true power of life and death. It wasn't just about how you appeared; it was more about how you operated. As he continued to hover outside the apothecary's workshop, he had a strange feeling that this encounter would forever change him, shaping him into a more skilful and knowledgeable assassin.

The decision point had finally arrived. He landed square on the windowsill, and the woman who was mixing potions turned to face him. She must have been nearly sixty, but her steely glare showed no signs of weakness or fear. She was clearly a force to be reckoned with, the scientist before science, cool, calm, and collected, even in the face of his unexpected and impossible intrusion.

"How did you get in here, and who are you?" Her voice was level and clear, cutting through the tension in the room.

Her cheekbones were high, her nose slightly pinched, and her eyes were so sharp they seemed to hold Jacob at knifepoint. The brief encounter stunned him. *Bad idea!* His mind chirped unhelpfully.

"I'm here to kill you, old witch!" His words were filled with venom, but his conviction was starting to waver.

She laughed, a sound that unmanned him and made him feel weak. She sat down casually on a nearby couch, far from the bench of potions. Her nonchalant response to Jacob's threat unnerved him further. Despite her age, she moved with a grace and elegance that defied her years.

"But you are just a boy. Why would you want to kill me?" Her question caught him off guard.

"Because you do evil things," he replied, trying to maintain a cool façade. But deep down, he knew he was in the presence of a superior being.

She studied him for a moment, her piercing gaze seemingly able to see through his every thought and emotion. "You are not the first to try and end my life, and you won't be the last," she laughed casually before replying in a sharper tone. "Anyway, what makes you think you have the right to judge me and my actions, child?"

Her words were like daggers, cutting deep into his conscience. How could he judge anyone, given what he was becoming? He struggled to find an answer to justify his actions, but the truth was, he couldn't. He was driven by blind hatred and a desire for revenge against Paulus, but in the face of this powerful woman, his conviction crumbled. He realised then that she was not the evil witch he had been led to believe. She was unusual, intriguing, and far more powerful than he could ever hope to be, although time would change that perception. With this realisation, a flood of emotions overwhelmed him: awe, fear, and a sense of shame for wanting to harm her.

He stood there, defeated and humbled but he couldn't help but admire the woman before him. She was a force of nature, a true master of her craft. In that moment, he knew he could never bring himself to harm her. He had come to kill, but instead, he found himself standing in the presence of a woman whom he could learn from, and his original plan dissolved, leaving him with no hand to play.

"How did you get in here, and who are you?" she said again, her voice low and clear, yet with a hint of curiosity.

"I saw the light burning and just climbed up," he said, still trying to understand his surprising new ability.

She instinctively knew that his last words were a lie, but also couldn't guess the truth, which gave her the uncanny feeling that her guest was somehow different from anyone she had known before. There was a slight aura of danger about him, but it was undeveloped, like that of a lion cub. His presence was unexpected, and she found herself lacking in physical defence against him. His cold stare and animalistic presence made her slightly uneasy, but she stood strong as he squatted like a bat in the unshuttered window.

"I'm here to... to... I am your death!" His voice was filled with anger but lacked conviction.

She laughed, unfazed by his threat, and calmly changed her position on the couch, giving him a scolding look. Jacob was stunned and suddenly felt silly squatting in the window like a constipated woodpecker.

"But why would you want to harm me? You do realise it is way past your bedtime." The words disarmed him further, and he felt the sting of embarrassment warm his cheeks as they flushed. She noted the subtle change with satisfaction. "It's clear you know what I do, but do you know why I do it? Why don't you come in? I will explain," she smiled maternally, and Jacob couldn't say no. One reason was because of the warmth he felt in her welcome that he had been missing all of his life, and the second was because he had no idea how to go back the way he had come without killing himself.

Jacob struggled down from the window ledge in an ungainly and awkward manner. He tried to regain some of his lost dignity by striking a nonchalant pose, leaning against the window frame with his arms folded across his chest and his legs crossed at the ankles.

"What do you mean?" he asked, suddenly feeling a sense of doubt creeping in. *So much for the "I am death" routine*, he thought. He felt his cheeks reddening further as he shifted uncomfortably.

"Would you like a drink?" She purred; her words slick as a cobra.

"No way!" he replied far too quickly, his posture snapped taut, standing up straight before self-consciously rearranging himself into an unconvincing slouch with one hand on his hip. "Okay, then why?" he asked, now genuinely curious.

"Because there is evil in this world, and some people do not have the strength or capacity to resist its embrace. So, I help the helpless," she answered, her words laced with wisdom and depth that only added to her mysterious character.

As she spoke, he couldn't help but feel a mix

of emotions: confusion, fear, and a strange sense of admiration for this woman who seemed to have a deeper purpose. He had never had a mother, and through it all, her voice remained rich and full of character, drawing him in even more.

Jacob felt he had met a kindred spirit in the mysterious poisoner, but his conscience still nagged at him. He couldn't shake the feeling that she was somehow responsible for the deaths of innocent people. How could he be drawn to someone who had caused so much harm? But then again, wasn't he guilty of the same? He had taken justice into his own hands and had acted as judge, jury, and executioner on several occasions already. Was he any better than her? As he considered her potential help, he couldn't help but feel a sense of betrayal towards his own values. *What values?* No morals there in the normal sense, but there was something good and honest hiding in his "kill or be killed" mentality.

He had always prided himself on being a moral and just person, but now he was considering seeking aid from a murderer. He quickly reminded himself that he was also a murderer and a thief as well, so he was technically worse than her. It didn't sit right with him on one hand, and he didn't want to dwell too much on his own crimes. Still, he couldn't deny that he needed her skills to achieve his own goals. As he thought about the levitation he had performed to gain entrance to her workshop, he felt a deep sense of unease. He also felt an acceleration of the weakening and knew that only human blood would enable him to remain strong and healthy. She would not be his next victim because she was nobody's fool and far too wily, easily outfoxing a string of previous emerging threats. Most had been dead before they got past the planning stage, owing to the clarity of her perception and deeply rooted survival instinct.

What had he become? How had he acquired such abilities? Was he becoming like her, using his powers for selfish purposes? The more he thought about it, the more he felt his resolve waning and self-doubt creep in like a spectre into the dark recesses of his mind. He had always prided himself on being in control, but now he was being pulled in two different directions. He wanted to maintain his moral compass, but he also wanted to achieve his goals. In the end, he knew he would have to make a choice, and it wasn't one he wanted to make. The thing was, he also couldn't deny the fascination the poisoner sparked in him, her expertise, and the quiet awe of her reputation. Jacob felt he had met a kindred spirit, but was disturbed by the fact that she did not fully assess who would be the victim of her poisons, and as a result, she had probably facilitated the murder of several innocents. He considered how she could help him. The weakening nagged at him again as it accelerated in him. It must have been exacerbated by the unexpected act of levitation he performed that had brought him into the poisoner's lair.

The pair conversed for what seemed like an eternity, their words intertwining and dancing in the air. With each passing moment, their mutual admiration and respect for one another only grew stronger. Jacob, with a glint of determination in his eyes, spoke of his time at the orphanage and how he had risen from the ashes of his past, becoming a force to be reckoned with. He spoke of his life in the orphanage, the difficulties he faced, and the unwavering strength he had developed to protect himself and the other children from the cruel hands of Paulus. Still, amidst the tales of his triumphs and tragedies, Jacob carefully omitted any mention of his true vampiric nature.

He knew the consequences of revealing his secret and was determined to keep it hidden, even from his newfound ally. In a moment of unexpected generosity, the poisoner offered Jacob a vial of her powerful potion, giving him the option to rid the orphanage of Paulus once and for all. However, Jacob, with a sly smile on his lips, had other plans, which he shared with the poisoner. He accepted the vial, knowing it would come in handy, but his true intentions were far more artful. He had asked her to prepare something less deadly but more devastating. A glint lit up her eyes, and the corner of her lip rose into a half smile as she nodded in agreement. As the conversation came to an end, Jacob left with a sense of satisfaction, knowing he had secured a valuable asset. The vial of precious liquid clutched tightly in his hand, he disappeared into the night, leaving the poisoner to ponder the true nature of the enigmatic visitor.

CHAPTER IX

The narrow streets were shrouded in a shadowy darkness, the kind that seemed to swallow everything in the absence of the moon. Jacob's throat was parched, but he knew better than to trust anyone who was a poisoner offering a drink. He knew of a fountain hidden down a narrow alleyway, a slight detour on his route back to the orphanage. The cool, refreshing water would quench his thirst, but to reach it, he had to navigate through the backstreets, a labyrinth of danger and deceit.

The only way to access the upper windows of the orphanage was to climb the treacherous back wall and precariously balance on the balcony before making a daring leap onto the gated staircase that barred the way to the dormitory. Once inside, he would not be able to get a drink until morning. Jacob's heart raced as he made his way towards the fountain, his senses on high alert. These streets were notorious for their dangers, and he knew that one wrong move could mean his death or enslavement.

The shadows seemed to shift and move, concealing hidden dangers lurking in every corner. As he turned a corner, Jacob caught a glimpse of two figures clad in red capes, their footsteps echoing ominously on the cobbled streets as they walked in unison. Two men, one set of footsteps. This order was out of place in this normally chaotic part of the town, especially when contrasted against the stillness of the night. Roman soldiers, on their nightly patrol. They moved with practised precision, and their equipment was meticulously maintained and strapped down carefully to ensure no unnecessary noise was made as they moved. Jacob couldn't help but feel a twinge of fear and awe at their formidable presence. There was no time to dwell on the pair of imposing figures, so he headed to the fountain before he was seen. Once he had slaked his thirst, he would get back to the orphanage before his absence was noticed.

With a burst of adrenaline, he darted towards his destination; the soldiers' measured footsteps faded into the distance behind him. The sound of water trickling greeted him as he finally reached the fountain, and he eagerly cupped his hands to take a sip. The cool liquid was like a balm to his parched throat, and he took a moment to relish the sensation. He knew he couldn't stay there for long. The absence of the soldiers meant that the area he was in would become more lawless with every receding step taken by the soldiers, and dangerous people would return at any moment. With one last long drink from the fountain, Jacob turned and made his way back into the darkness, his heart pounding with trepidation. The local people were not stupid and were astutely aware of the patrol routes the soldiers took and the time it took them to perform them. The Roman army was a well-oiled machine, but the locals were also like an army. An army of ants.

Jacob felt the weakening stab at him again, his newfound confidence beginning to drain away as he negotiated the labyrinth of dangerous streets. He was thirsty for blood, but the thought of targeting another victim filled him with guilt and disgust. He knew what he was doing was wrong, but the thrill of the chase and control over another human being was too enticing to resist, especially as it empowered him so much.

As he walked, he noticed a prostitute in a dark doorway, beckoning to him lewdly. A voice in his head whispered, *why not her?* But Jacob knew he couldn't bring himself to harm someone who had already suffered so much. She deserved better than to be another one of his victims after such a short time on the planet, trapped in a life of misery. *Why not her?* He asked himself again, feeling the pull of his twisted desires. He could feel the weakening clawing at his strength, tempting him to give in to his darkest urges. He fought against it, but the voice grew louder, urging him on. *Why not her?* It repeated, his mind clouded with conflicting thoughts.

Because she's human, just like me. Or am I? Because she deserves a chance at a better life. Because I can't keep living with this guilt and shame. But the voice wouldn't be silenced. *Why not her?* It taunted, pushing Jacob to the brink. He could feel himself losing control, his mind spinning with indecision and turmoil. *WHY NOT HER???* He finally gave in, succumbing to the darkness within him. He reached for the woman, his hand shaking with fear and excitement. He knew he was making a very bad choice, but he couldn't stop himself. He was consumed by his own inner demons, unable to resist their temptations and demands.

As he drew closer to the girl, he could see the fear and resignation in her eyes. She suddenly looked incredibly weak and vulnerable. He knew he would regret this moment for the rest of his life, but he was powerless to stop it. The weakening had won the savage battle of wits, and Jacob was losing the ability to care about the consequences of his actions. Abruptly, he turned down another alleyway, physically diverting his own attack. He let out a deep breath, and his hands were shaking. *I'm never doing that! He said to himself. Cage the beast, you fool! Don't become what you hate.* This was a difficult thought for a natural killer. *Just because you like to eat meat does not mean you should torture animals,* he chided himself gently as the intense feelings began to subside.

What was I thinking? His quick pace gradually slowed, and a deep sense of guilt and shame settled over him. He could feel the weight of his own bare feet as they made progress towards the orphanage; the sound of them slapping the ground echoed through the gloomy cobbled streets. Lost in a stormy sea of contradictory emotions, Jacob was consumed by the intensity of his own conflicting thoughts.

Suddenly, a hand shot out of the shadows. His body was wrenched by a rough hand that seized his tunic, and a couple of clumsy blows bounced off his skull before he was smashed into the wall; his head struck the stone savagely, and it stunned him. As he was roughly pushed up against the wall of a narrow alley, his blood began to boil with unrestrained fury. He had been ready to kill and was trying to suppress it, so it did not take much for his wrath to release itself from Jacob's tenuous grip on self-control. He could feel the fierce desire for revenge burning within him, and new bruises were already rising on his head and face. With a sudden burst of energy, Jacob regained his composure and head-butted his assailant violently, breaking his nose before he could even utter a single threat.

A loud slurping noise escaped his mouth as Jacob wrapped his mouth around the man's heavily bleeding nose, and he couldn't help but feel a twisted sense of amusement at the cross-eyed look of shock on his victim's face. He laughed, and as he did, the attacker's eyes betrayed a sense of pure terror. Jacob's amusement quickly faded as his grip tightened around the man's hair. He punched him in the throat, crushing his windpipe, silencing and asphyxiating him in one swift motion. As his attacker's body fell limp in his arms, Jacob couldn't help but feel a sense of satisfaction at the look of fear and pain on the man's face. The darkness within him had been unleashed, and he knew he would feed his blood lust that night. He would regain his strength and conquer the weakening with this man's lifeblood. The conflicting emotions continued to rage within him, but for now, he was simply grateful to be alive as he bit deeply into the jugular of the prostrate figure lying on the ground, who twitched and spasmed in the final throes of asphyxiation and blood loss. He fed deeply, taking care to avoid bloodying himself.

His confidence and strength had returned with a fiery determination by the time he reached the orphanage. The haunting memories of his weakness were now mere whispers in the back of his mind, easily drowned out by his renewed sense of purpose. He stood before the towering wall behind the orphanage, ready to scale it with ease, but then, a daring thought crossed his mind. Could he replicate his previous levitation trick? With a confident stride, he approached the gated stairs, unsure of what to expect as he came face to face with the imposing gates. He was not one to back down from a challenge. With a fierce determination, he willed himself to rise over the gates and onto the upper part of the stairwell, where the dormitory awaited. Just like before, a surge of power coursed through his body, filling him with a euphoric rush as he rose up towards the sky, clearing the gates with ease. "Upwards and onwards," he said to himself as he landed halfway up the staircase that served as one of the main access routes to the dormitory during the daylight hours. A wicked grin lit his features as he took his first step up the staircase towards the door.

As he entered the dormitory, his senses came alive. The soft snores of Paulus welcomed him, his mouth slightly open as he slept. Jacob reached into his pocket and retrieved a small vial, its contents a potent elixir that would rob Paulus of his strength. With precision, he let a single drop fall onto Paulus' tongue. Paulus stirred slightly, wrinkling his nose and licking his lips before swallowing the elixir. Satisfied that the bullying arsehole had ingested it, Jacob shook him gently awake. Instantly, terror flooded Paulus' expression, and his heart pounded in his chest. He instinctively looked down, half expecting to see flames crawling up his body. But instead, he saw only the cruel determination in Jacob's eyes and felt a tight sickness in his stomach. His mouth went dry, and he tried to generate some saliva by working his tongue.

"What do you want?" Paulus hissed, trying to push Jacob away and wincing as pain shot through his recently broken finger.

"I was just checking to ensure you are getting your beauty sleep, darling," Jacob said in a concerned parental voice.

Anger replaced the fear. "I was asleep, you bastard," spat Paulus.

"This is two!" Jacob said, holding up two fingers. "Unfortunately, you are going to have a shit time, darling. You really should try to get some sleep now; you are keeping the little ones awake with your whining."

The raised voices had woken most of the others, and murmurs of "Has he pissed the bed again?" could clearly be heard amongst the younger ones, who were proud that they hadn't. All of the children had heard Jacob's words and giggled at the way Jacob called Paulus "darling." As Jacob settled down to sleep, emboldened by the darkness, a cute little voice called out: "Good night, darling!" And the whole dormitory burst into loud and unrestrained laughter, with the odd giggling fit breaking out sporadically; it had begun to grow light before it fully subsided.

CHAPTER X

The orphanage was a far cry from the pleasant home of his childhood. Paulus lay awake that night, listening to the gurgling in his belly. If that wasn't enough, the younger brats were constantly giggling at his expense. He silently vowed to make them all pay. Despite his displeasure at the situation, he managed to fall into a fitful sleep. When he awoke, the staff were already calling the orphans to start a new day.

It was difficult to pry himself away from the pleasures of sleep; his mattress was so warm, soft, and inviting, but it had a pungent smell. What is that? He thought dreamily. The cramp that suddenly clutched his belly was so violent that his hand automatically flew to clutch it. As the spasm passed, his hand encountered something warm and sloppy. Bringing his hand up to his face, he realised with horror that it was covered in shit. The smell was overwhelming, and he couldn't help but gag. As he did so, his stomach cramped violently, and he lost control of his bowels for the second time in hours. This time, he was fully conscious.

The shame was crushing, and before he could even process what was happening, the urchin in the next bed, who had just witnessed the whole thing, yelled, "He's only gone and shit the bed now! Ughhh!"

Within seconds, a crowd of small children

had surrounded his bed, all holding their noses and making sounds of disgust. Paulus could feel the weight of their judgment, which just added to his embarrassment, and he wanted them all to disappear. It took several minutes before the staff could usher the unruly bunch to the canteen. Paulus lay there, feeling utterly humiliated and wishing that this nightmare would finally be over. Jacob was one of the last to leave the dormitory, having helped the staff round up some of the smaller ones.

"Sorry you are having such a shit time, darling," he said, out of earshot of the staff, before quietly leaving the room.

After Paulus' unexpected fall from grace, Jacob's days in the orphanage were filled with diligent studies and daily chores. His education was thorough, and he excelled in reading and writing. He was particularly gifted in Aramaic and was quickly mastering the Latin language as well. The Orphanage Director had wisely added Latin to the curriculum, knowing that fluency in the language would give the orphans a competitive edge in the ever-expanding Roman Empire.

With his daily tasks completed, the young Jacob decided to take a walk down to the river to clear his mind. Despite the heat and fatigue from a long day, Jacob couldn't help but smile to himself as he recalled the events of the previous night. He had stood up to Paulus, the notorious bully of the orphanage, and had emerged victorious. For so long, Paulus had been the scourge of the orphanage, but now Jacob had exposed him for the coward he truly was. As he strolled along the riverbank, Jacob's thoughts turned to his future. With his education and newfound confidence, he was determined to make something of himself and leave the orphanage behind.

He saw Josh and his cousin John frolicking in the water. He heard them before he saw them and just followed the river down to the source of the cacophony. They seemed to be having a great time, splashing each other and fighting in a good-natured way, trying to dunk each other. It was funny but weird as the winner of each dunking competition would yell, "I forgive you," and both would burst into laughter, diving and swimming in the shallows. John took a huge run-up from a high bank and screamed, "I forgive myself!" before hitting the river surface in a massive explosion of water, only to rise to the surface to catch a quick breath before Josh shouted, "I forgive you too!" before driving him back under the water with a howl of laughter. It seemed like a great game, and Jacob joined in fully, the thoughts of the poisoner, Paulus, and the orphanage lost to him for the time being as the trio splashed and grappled in the water. The best jump competition came next as the boys climbed out of the river and made their way to a particularly high bank.

Throwing off his tunic, dressed only in his loin cloth, Jacob ran to the bank, performed a somersault, and then just hung in the air for three full seconds before plunging into the deliciously cold waters of the river. Josh and John looked at each other, surprised by this unusual sight.

"I don't know what happened there," Jacob said, shrugging.

"And I thought I was weird," Josh laughed.

The game continued unabated until all three were worn out and hungry. Lying on the grass with his young friends, Jacob felt an amazing sense of tranquillity descend over him.

"How's life in the orphanage?" Josh asked.

"Getting better. I have bested that horrible bully Paulus. Not only that, but I have also made him look so shitty to the other orphans that he is less of a tyrant to them. They mock him from the shadows now. It's actually quite funny. They are free from his control," Jacob laughed with a mischievous glint in his eye.

"Yes, you seem to have grown into a man over a short space of time. It's good that the orphanage is more peaceful," Josh said, adding, "Blessed are the peacemakers."

"I did not make peace; I made war. Bullshit to the peacemakers, I say! It was not violent, well, not very violent. Still, the little ones are safer now," said Jacob triumphantly.

"Well, these are your choices on which you

will ultimately be judged," Josh stated, looking mildly concerned and yet pious at the same time.

"The thing is, Josh, I'm more of an 'eye for an eye' type of guy. If you turn the other cheek in the orphanage, the other cheek will get slapped twice as hard whilst someone else runs off with your sandals," laughed Jacob. He continued, "So you know how you are always banging on about sheep and wolves? What if I were a wolf in sheep's clothing, protecting the flock?"

"Yes, I can see that working," Josh said thoughtfully, looking towards a nearby olive tree and rubbing his chin. "Nice expression; I might use it, would you mind?"

"No worries. Words are free, my friend," Jacob said, hurrying on to get to his next point. It was good to speak to people who did not share his claustrophobic and insidious environment, although he often found it strange how complacent they were when it came to the basics of life. They lived in peace, so they talked about peace. They ate in peace, slept in peace, and everything was exactly where they had left it when they woke up the next morning.

"Anyway, I'm nearly a man now. I will be evicted from the orphanage within the year, and I will need some form of employment. I'm really not sure what to do," Jacob concluded with a shrug.

Josh looked around him and gestured at the

river, the trees, and the burning land shimmering in the heat. "Everything is there for the taking, and every decision is just yes or no; after that, it is truly your choice, and your actions will be seen as just or unjust. You must be true to your soul." This left Jacob feeling somewhat conflicted as a murderer, poisoner, and liberator.

"Why do you always talk in riddles?" asked Jacob.

"So, the message will pass on, but wrongdoers will not be able to use my words as a weapon. They will, but it softens the impact if they are slightly inscrutable."

"A big claim for a table maker," laughed Jacob. "Seriously though, what am I going to do for a living? Do you know of anyone looking for an apprentice?"

"Ask, and it will be given; seek, and you shall find; knock, and the door will be opened to you," said Josh.

Jacob laughed as he charged back to the river. "So basically, work it out for myself then?" He shouted as he leapt from the high bank.

"Pretty much!" yelled Josh just before he hit the water, swiftly followed by John shouting, "I forgive everyone!"

The three stayed by the river until it grew dark, laughing and having fun because they were

young and did not appreciate the deadly challenges
they all would face in the coming years.

CHAPTER XI

Jacob's return to the orphanage presented a familiar scene, as he had spent all of his life there. His mind was preoccupied with thoughts of his future; as a young man, he knew that his time in the orphanage would soon be over. This knowledge led to mixed thoughts and swirling emotions. His reverie was interrupted by the sound of Paulus being returned to the dormitory by the staff. Jacob couldn't help but feel hate for Paulus, knowing that the orphanage was not a kind place, especially for those who could not take care of themselves. As he watched Paulus being led to his bed, Jacob thought about the harsh realities of life. He knew that he would have to work hard to survive in the outside world. His mind drifted to the conversation he had with Josh earlier that day when he had used the phrase "a wolf in sheep's clothing" whilst trying to make his own troubled existence fit with Josh's beliefs. Jacob found the phrase to be quite poetic and was flattered when Josh asked if he could use it.

"No worries, words are free, my friend," he had replied. Little did he know that this phrase would stick with him and serve as a reminder of his future responsibilities. As he settled back into his bed, Jacob couldn't shake his deep sense of anxiety about the uncertainty of his future. He did not know what he would do, but he was determined to make it on his own. His time at the orphanage had taught him the value of hard work and perseverance, and he was ready to face whatever challenges lay ahead. Worst of all, he knew he would still need to kill to live, and that act could easily lead to crucifixion or even stoning.

He tried to sleep, but anxiety plagued him. Josh once told him that: "The devil makes work for idle hands." And his hands were certainly idle now. A sense of mischief rose within him. Thoughts of the math classes he had taken in the orphanage took on a new and dangerous aspect. He decided to break his own rules.

Quietly, taking the vial the poisoner had given him, he tiptoed towards Paulus' bed. The snores and nocturnal moans of the orphans were the orchestra of the night. Paulus slept in his usual way, mouth slightly open and a gentle snore rolling in his throat. One drop released from the vial fell into Paulus' mouth. His nose wrinkled; his mouth worked as if he was chewing.

When Jacob was sure that the laxative had been digested, he leaned in.

"What do you think about fractions, darling?"

"Huh?" Paulus responded groggily.

"Personally, I prefer decimals; which one do you prefer?"

"What?" Paulus' mind raced, trying to make sense of the bizarre conversation. There was the seed of relief in his mind that this might be the final act of retribution from Jacob, whom he had persecuted so relentlessly in his younger years. He just wanted it to end.

"Fractions, I prefer fractions!"

"Okay, this is two and a half shitty arse," Jacob crooned. "2.5, just so you are clear, darling. Have a shit day."

After the previous embarrassment, Paulus did not want to repeat the horrendous experience of being found in bed covered in shit as his former victims mocked him. He got out of bed and headed to the latrines, where he rode the waves of revenge that Jacob had dealt him for the rest of the night and most of the next day. Every time he thought it was over and attempted to return to the dormitory, the urgent call from his bowels sent him scurrying back to the latrines. Finally, when it was over, he felt exhausted but resolved himself to speak to the staff and report that Jacob had been poisoning him.

The Director of the orphanage was a kind man, but his eyes held a hardness that betrayed the years of witnessing unspeakable acts of cruelty. Outside, the locals still called him the "Orphan Keeper." Miriam and Leah had long since moved on. He had heard it all and seen it all before: the cries of agony, the pleas for mercy, the shattered innocence. His hair was now shot through with streaks of grey.

Paulus, with his slick words and charming façade, was just another in a long line of manipulators who preyed on the vulnerable. The Director was no fool; he saw through Paulus' façade, recognising the same darkness that lurked within so many other lost souls. It was the desire to boost one's own ego by destroying the self-worth and well-being of others. Years of working with orphans had honed the Director's instincts, making him an astute judge of character with a sixth sense for lies.

The Director and his staff could sense the fear and desperation in the orphans, and he knew how to calm their trembling souls. However, Paulus was different; his twisted mind revelled in their suffering, relishing in the power he held over them. The Director had little sympathy for such a despicable child. Still, he reminded himself to remain impartial, to judge each incident without bias or favour. It was a difficult task to put aside his personal feelings and see the truth with clarity, but the orphans were counting on him, and he would not let them down.

With a heavy heart, he steeled himself for yet another battle against the darkness that threatened to upset the delicate balance of his institution. When he spoke, the Director's voice was rich with experience and wisdom, and it carried the weight of the countless stories he had witnessed and participated in. Every word was imbued with a deep perception of the institution he ran and its occupants, evoking a sense of empathy and determination. His character held a depth that could not be easily fathomed. As he stood before Paulus, his gaze unflinching and his voice unwavering, it was clear that he was as unmoveable as the great pyramids that peppered Egypt. No child's argument could blind him to the facts, and he was a master at uncovering truths in the vast desert of lies. Paulus had told the Director of his suspicions of what he thought Jacob had done to him clumsily, and he had overplayed it too much, making the Director doubt him.

"Okay, Paulus, we will investigate," the Director said tonelessly. "But you must know that if I find this claim false, misleading, or with a questionable motive, you will be beaten."

"Spare the rod, spoil the child." It was one of his favourite sayings.

"I understand, but he is trying to kill me," whined Paulus.

"Is that an accusation or a loose thought?"

"Jacob is evil. He never used to be, but he just changed from a skinny little runt to a beast in a few months. He is sly and dangerous. He is vindictive, and there is something that has changed in his eyes, and..."

"You have not exactly been kind to him, though, have you, Paulus?" the Director stated factually.

"No, but he has a vendetta; he is persecuting me. He is not human!"

"Mmmm, relax, that's a bit far," said the Director flatly. "Get a grip on reality, and you reap what you sow, Paulus. This may be the most important lesson of your life. You should treat people as you wish to be treated."

"What about David and Goliath?"

"You misunderstand the story. When what happened to Goliath happens to you, come to my office and complain about it then. I will investigate, but I hope you have learned a lesson. It seems that you pick on the meek and abuse them in your cruel games. It also seems that some of the meek are not so meek now. Go back to the Dorm; I will send for you when I have concluded my enquiries."

Paulus' bowels contracted, and he left the principal's room quickly. Later that night, Paulus approached Jacob's bed as he slept. *Two can play at this game.* He thought. He grabbed Jacob roughly by the throat to prevent any noise. He slapped Jacob hard in the face. The sound woke some of the smaller urchins.

"I have reported you to the principal for poisoning, and the punishment for that is stoning!"

Jacob was shocked from his slumber by the slap but strangely felt a sense of calm. An unassailable power ran through his veins. As Paulus began to rant, Jacob could see the thick veins stand out in his meaty forearms. He seized Paulus' arm in a surprisingly powerful grip, bit deeply, and drank greedily. The dominance in Paulus' eyes was quickly replaced by fear, and he tried to withdraw. It was useless, and Jacob's teeth remained fully engaged, held in place by the powerful grip that he had established on Paulus' arm. Horrified, Paulus bolted backwards in a desperate attempt to escape. As he did so, Jacob was dragged out of the bed and across the floor. He remained obscenely attached, sucking blood from Paulus' veins as he bumped over the bare wooded floorboards, making slurping sounds as he went.

A few orphans grew scared but kept quiet, somehow understanding that this was the last battle in an epic conflict. However, they had no idea that Jacob would continue to fight long after their deaths, in conflicts of such magnitude that they could never imagine. Finally, Jacob released his grip on Paulus, allowing him to leap into his bed, where he comically pulled the blanket over his head like an infant trying to escape a nightmare.

"Thanks for breakfast, darling," Jacob said smoothly as he walked back to his bed.

"Night, darling," a little voice shouted, and the dormitory erupted in laughter again as the blood around Jacob's mouth remained shrouded in darkness, screening his secret from the others. Paulus knew he could not remain in the place where he felt victimised, and the shame and despair of defeat just compounded his misery.

CHAPTER XII

J acob was at a crossroads. He had trudged his way through life in the orphanage for years and had seen his fair share of desperation, brutality, and fear. Paulus' situation was no different, yet Jacob found himself struggling with feelings of sympathy towards him. He had become an astute judge of character, having spent his whole life surviving in a chaotic sea of orphans against a background of swift and brutal discipline from the staff and a consistent bullying culture amongst the children in which only the strong could survive. As a result of this, he was determined not to let these emotions cloud his judgment; if it were the other way around, Paulus would not have afforded Jacob any sympathy.

He knew that he must bring the situation to its ultimate conclusion. Despite his best efforts, Jacob couldn't shake off the memories of Paulus' constant pleas and petitions to the Director. He knew it was only a matter of time before Paulus' desperation would reach a boiling point, resulting in fingers being pointed strongly in his own direction. Jacob had noticed the toll it was taking on Paulus; his sleep had been disturbed, and he looked tired and agitated. He was short and sharp with the other orphans but dared not hit them anymore. In turn, the smaller ones knew this, and their mockery became bolder by the day as they dared each other to provoke the sullen bully more and more. It was just a matter of time until Paulus reacted. Jacob knew that a cornered animal was the most dangerous and that it was better to kill it or let it escape than allow it to strike.

It worried him, knowing that the vial was hidden outside the orphanage, and he was concerned that it would be found and somehow linked to him, proving the accusations made by Paulus. It was a constant burden on his shoulders, as its discovery could lead to his death. Still, Jacob couldn't help but feel a sense of relief that the vial was not stored within the orphanage. He knew that it would bring nothing but chaos and destruction if it were to fall into the wrong hands. However, the thought of it being discovered bothered him deeply, and it began to wear abrasively on his nerves, destroying his peace of mind. Too many loose ends, too much of a ragged tear. It became apparent that it was time to end the game. End the chase and go for the kill. He also knew that he had to divert the attention of the Director from the accusations Paulus constantly made against him before any of them stuck. One more throw of the dice and he would end his sick little game along with Paulus' earthly existence.

The orphanage was supported by charity, and often, the staff and smaller children would go into the streets with begging bowls. The staff liked to take the younger ones out to raise funds as they garnered more sympathy with their big eyes and chubby cheeks. They pulled in more money than a bunch of surly teenagers would, and so the orphanage was as rich or poor as the hearts of strangers. The coin was kept in the Director's office, in a big chest, and his office was at the end of the corridor, with a large window to allow for some ventilation. The office was sacrosanct, and no one entered freely but the Director himself; everyone else was summoned. It was a sacred and mystical place, the great unknown. From this room, the Director bought food for the orphans and managed the fabric of the buildings. An attack on this place would be taken personally by the Director, regardless of his attempted self-regulation and professionalism. It would be seen as beyond personal, as he would see it as an attack on the vulnerable children in his care.

Perfect, Jacob thought as he looked across the dormitory at Paulus' sleeping form. He quietly arose from his bed and made his way to Paulus' bed. He shook his shoulder gently.

"You will have a nice day tomorrow. Have a break, but don't hurt anyone." The familiar fear was evident in Paulus' eyes and was slowly replaced by confusion.

"Number three can wait," Jacob said harshly. The fear quickly replaced the confusion in Paulus' eyes. His mind raced; why did Jacob always talk in riddles? He thought he was almost as stupid as that kid Josh, with whom he was always hanging around. Was this a threat, or was it a genuine respite from persecution? I will have to kill him, Paulus said to himself. He slept well that night and drifted off, imagining brutal ways to end Jacob's time on Earth.

The next day was relatively calm in the orphanage, and Jacob was good to his word. A couple of young ones had a ragged little battle at lunchtime, which the staff ended effectively with a few strikes of the stick. It started when one of the little urchins made a joke about another child's mother, knowing that none of them had one. Dark humour harmed as much as it helped, and was a common coping mechanism among the orphans.

"I haven't got a mother!" the little one screamed, the sadness and desperation etched into his face. "And neither have you."

"I know; that is why it is so funny!" The last provocation was too much; the little one's temper snapped, and they went at each other without a check.

Jacob looked away. It was a hard environment, and he knew he would leave it soon, but was unsure how he could look after himself alone in the big wide world. He realised that he had become institutionalised and must become independent. He had to get out. In a strange way, he only realised this because his vampirism had forced him to become more independent. He had to rely on his own wits to survive, and there was no one he could talk to about his deadly nocturnal activities outside of the orphanage. They did not serve blood in the canteen, so he had to find his own. Suddenly, the thought of blood brought on the first pangs of weakening. He looked over at Paulus and licked his lips. It was time to end the game.

CHAPTER XIII

That night, Jacob left the dormitory quietly. He effortlessly levitated over the locked gate and rounded the orphanage until he stood outside the end of the building that housed the Director's office. *Up!* he said in his mind and felt the now familiar sensation running down his spine as he floated up towards the Director's office window. The shutters were closed, and he was relieved to find that they were not locked. He tried to open the shutter quietly, but the hinge squeaked. It was not loud, but in his precarious position, it sounded like an earthquake to him. He froze and then considered his actions. Being still on the window ledge of the Director's office held no advantage. There would be no way to explain his actions. *Get in. Get out. Complete the task*, he said to himself.

Jacob moved fast and effectively through the window and strove to find the money chest. He laid his feet gently and moved in silence. He was horrendously aware of his own beating heart and the sound of his breath; he made a conscious effort to calm both. Strangely, he felt a sense of calm descend on him as he entered what would later be known as a flow state, elevating his confidence. *I'm scared, but I am not scared even though I am doing scary things*, he smirked as the thought ran through his mind. *This is because you have been hanging out with a poisoner!* His mind added uninvited. Having found the chest, he took thirty pieces of silver, not realising that this would become known as the traitor's price for millennia, as it would sure as hell nail Josh to a cross because his views ran contrary to those of the mighty Roman Empire. His vision would continue beyond him to create peace and war in equal measure; it would aid and arrest human progress as time ran its relentless course. Still, Jacob could not see the future. At this point, he was still blissfully unaware of the curse of his own immortality that would lead him to experience the inexorable progress and regress of human technology, society, and the resulting conflicts over the next two thousand years. His heart hammered in his chest as his mind raced with the consequences of being caught in the act as he raided the coffers of the orphanage.

He gathered the coins into a small bag he had brought for the purpose and felt a sense of guilt. This was theft. He did not like that, but he justified his actions by telling himself that he was committing it on behalf of Paulus, who would receive severe punishment from the Director. It was poetic justice; he had to be the wolf in order to protect the little lambs that resided in the orphanage. He had sensed Paulus was becoming a threat, and he had learned the hard way to trust his instincts in growing up in the merciless orphanage. The threat needed to be neutralised and removed.

As he descended towards the floor, content the shutter had been closed properly. He knew what he had to do immediately, but was suddenly unsure if his plan would succeed. There was still an awful lot that could go wrong. *I'm getting good at that*, he thought as he landed smoothly and smiled to himself. He quickly made his way back to the living quarters and leapt over the locked gate in a way that was partly athletic and partly levitation. That was weird, he thought, but he was quickly becoming accustomed to "Wierd," a word that would not arrive in his vocabulary until the time of the Vikings. Unusual was the nearest translation. Once again, he was unaware that in the future, he would learn to speak languages that did not yet exist and master technologies that were not yet even ideas, but for now, he was just focused on ending the deadly conflict that he and Paulus were engaged in.

He had retrieved the vial from its hiding place on his way back to the dormitory that the poisoner had made for him. Paulus was snoring softly, as usual, mouth slightly open. It was an alluring target for a poisoner as much as it was for a vampire. *Choices, choices.* Jacob quietly placed the bag of silver under Paulus' mattress at waist level. He allowed a droplet of the potion to fall from the vial into Paulus' mouth, he administered another drop, and then a third. He watched as Paulus' face did its usual twitching as his mouth worked and his nose wrinkled. Once certain the high dose had been fully ingested, he gently woke Paulus.

"You will be in the shit tomorrow, darling,

your holiday is over. This is number three."

"Fuck off and leave me alone!" Paulus whispered aggressively.

"No, you will fuck off, and you will leave us all alone," smiled Jacob with cold eyes.

As soon as it was light, Jacob left the orphanage before the children had been woken by the staff. The smell of Paulus' self-soiling was already thick in the air. He wanted to make sure the vial disappeared before Paulus was discovered. As he walked into the town, he watched an Optio of the Roman Army begin to delegate his Centurion's orders to his century, a military formation that misleadingly contained roughly eighty men. They always started their patrols from the well, nearest to the market to ensure that their men were fully hydrated and that their water skins were full. Once again, Jacob was impressed by their discipline, order, and sense of purpose. He suddenly realised this was his escape. He was tall enough, over two inches over the basic requirement. He was fit, and he had lived in an orphanage all of his life. Surely, that must be tougher than any barrack block, where soldiers strove to support each other, unlike the orphanage, where it was a constant all-out war in which only the strong could survive. The Optio had finished giving his orders, and all the patrols had been deployed. The Centurion stood on strong legs which were widely planted. His arms were muscular and crossed as he nodded in an authoritarian but friendly way as the

Optio explained the reasons that had inspired his strategy to his superior.

"We found another dead one the other day. Broken nose, and it looked like there were teeth marks on it also."

"The plebs around here are fucking mental, mate." The Centurion grunted. "Please send me back to Spain." The Centurion laughed. "The civvies out there are nicer and more civilised than in this god-forsaken place."

The Optio interrupted him. "Sir, the man had no blood in him and two holes in his neck."

"An aggressive whore." The Centurion laughed.

"No, Sir. You know when you go on campaign, and a man is hit in the femoral artery or the jugular or when they just bleed inside of themselves?"

"Been having nightmares?" He laughed. "We all do, Optio; it comes with the job."

"No, but this one was not normal. It wasn't your usual stabbing, strangling, or beating. It was very unusual, and this is why I have changed the patrol patterns."

"Fair play, mate. Well done."

Their conversation was interrupted by the approach of an athletic-looking young man with enigmatic eyes.

"Excuse me!" said the stranger. He was a local, and both soldiers immediately assumed a military bearing. Not aggressive but ready. His clothes were shabby, but his movements were lithe, almost like those of the lions that the Centurion had watched devour the men unlucky enough to share the amphitheatre floor with them.

"What is the matter, son, are you lost?" The Centurion said curtly, shaking the memories of men being dismembered as the crowd cheered with savage glee.

"How can I join?" Jacob had not intended to blurt it out but to engage the soldiers in questions about their lives. However, their presence intimidated him, and the words had clumsily escaped before he could stop them.

"You're a cocky little shit, aren't you, boy!" the Centurion bellowed in his parade square voice, forcing Jacob to take a step back. "Stand still! Let's have a look at you."

The Centurion stepped back and made no attempt to hide his appraisal of Jacob's physique. The Optio weighed up the youth's ability to carry heavy weights over long distances and came to the conclusion that he probably could, before reminding himself of the strong-looking individuals who failed during his selection week, as some of the weaker-looking candidates had aced it. With soldiers, *you just can't judge a book by its cover*, he thought.

The Optio remembered a chubby bloke in basic training who could outrun all of the Physical Training Instructors, resulting in horrendous runs and forced marches over months that everyone had to suffer. He remembered throwing up and having to keep running whilst the instructors tried to establish their physical superiority over Fat Claudius, who never cared anyway but always arrived at the finish line first. He turned his head and spat at the memory. The kid would have to sink or swim. He was a know-nothing, done-nothing, who could be nothing more until he passed selection.

"How old are you?"

Jacob did not know his exact birthday, but just said "Seventeen," because he knew that was the minimum joining age.

"Okay, come here tomorrow at noon. We will find out when the next selection process takes place and let you know."

"Okay, see you then. Here, tomorrow at noon," Jacob said meekly as he turned to walk away, his heart beating hard in his chest.

"Don't be late!" the Optio commanded.

"I will be waiting here at noon tomorrow, Sir," Jacob said with far more conviction than he felt.

"Don't call me Sir, I work for a living!" The Optio yelled, somewhat confusingly. "Now fuck off until tomorrow."

"Okay, thanks," Jacob said and gave a little wave, which he immediately regretted as he turned and walked away in a cloud of embarrassment and shame. It certainly hadn't gone the way he planned it, but it was a start.

"What do you think?" The Centurion asked his Optio.

"He didn't claim to be the world's strongest man, which is always a good sign." The Optio scratched his chin. "He will either pass selection or he won't, probably won't even show up."

The Centurion scanned his environment. "Whatever, see what happens. They are all fucking crazy out here anyway."

Jacob found Josh sitting in the bustling plaza; the sounds of merchants shouting and coins clinking filled the air. He approached his friend with trepidation, knowing the weight of his decision would be met with disapproval.

"I'm leaving the orphanage," Jacob spoke with a steely determination, his voice devoid of any emotion. "It is time for a new beginning." Little did he know that those words would haunt him for centuries to come.

Josh's eyes widened in shock, a mixture of concern and disbelief written across his face. "What will you do?" he asked, his voice tinged with care and concern.

"I'm joining the Roman Army as an Auxiliary," Jacob declared, his jaw set stubbornly.

"No!" Josh exclaimed, his voice rising in intensity. "They are godless, evil people who will never change their ways. Crucifixions, murderous games, and endless wars for conquest. Is that the life you want? Do you really want to be part of that?"

"It's better than being a sheep," Jacob argued, his words laced with bitterness.

"But you could be a shepherd," Josh countered, his voice gentle yet firm. "Someone who guides and protects their flock."

Jacob scoffed, his voice dripping with disdain. "And who are the shepherd's best friends? Sheep, that's who. I'd still be stuck with the same flock."

"So, you're going to join a pack of wolves?" Josh questioned, his eyes searching Jacob's face for any sign of doubt.

"How do you know I am not a wolf already?" Jacob retorted, his tone challenging and cryptic.

As Jacob walked away, Josh couldn't help but feel a sense of unease. His friend was changing before his very eyes, becoming someone he barely recognised. He couldn't shake the feeling that this decision would lead Jacob down a dangerous and unpredictable path, whilst being ironically unaware of the dangers he was also courting as a result of his ever-increasing revolutionary rhetoric and the growing suspicions of the Romans.

CHAPTER XIV

Upon returning to the orphanage, it was blatantly obvious that Paulus' wrongdoing had been uncovered. It appeared that Paulus' ailment had resurfaced with a vengeance. Despite his obvious illness, the staff showed little compassion for the semi-conscious young man who lay writhing in his own filth. They were well aware that this was not the first time they had to clean up such a horrendous mess. As Paulus was escorted to the medical wing, barely able to remain on his feet, two other staff members began to strip the bed. The bedding would have to be incinerated. As the mattress was lifted, a small bag spilt its contents onto the bare wooden boards, making a dull clattering sound. The two helpers exchanged shocked and surprised glances.

"We need to get the Director!" they exclaimed in unison.

The Director had refused to enter the dormitory, and now the unsoiled bag and its silver contents sat on his desk, revealing Paulus' true nature as a thief. The Director's decision was clear: when Paulus recovered, his punishment would be severe and irreversible. The room was silent except for the sound of the silver items being placed one by one on the table. The two helpers exchanged worried looks, knowing that the Director's wrath would be unleashed upon Paulus.

The stolen items glinted in the dim light, a stark contrast to the bare and worn wooden boards of the dormitory onto which they had originally fallen. The Director's desk, usually a symbol of authority and organisation, now held evidence of an orphan's selfish crime. The staff knew that this discovery would have serious consequences, not just for Paulus, but could have jeopardised the orphanage's ability to look after the orphans. The office was usually a place of order and calm, but now it was filled with tension and anger. The stolen items were now carefully laid out on his desk, each one a reminder of Paulus' deceitful actions. The Director's mind raced with thoughts of how to best handle this situation and how to teach Paulus a lesson he would never forget. He needed to set an example. As the sun set outside, the orphanage was filled with whispers and rumours about Paulus' theft. The Director's decision weighed heavily on everyone's mind, and they could only wait and see what would happen next.

The next morning was full of tension. Meetings were held with the Director and the staff before sunrise, and neither the children nor the staff had slept well that night. They were not discussions, though; they were instructional. There needed to be a point made, and it had to be made in the strongest possible way. Contingencies were arranged in the solemn atmosphere, as were other procedures which depended on the outcome of the sentence to be inflicted. All orphans were ordered to the central area that served as a playground at dawn. There would be no play today. Paulus had been strapped to a waist-high cross and was kneeling down in front of it, his legs and tunic stained with smudges of excrement.

The Director stood off to the side in his awkward and gangly way, his eyes bulging ominously. He looked like he had aged much more than the seventeen years from when Jacob had been dumped into his care. He did not like violence, but sometimes it was necessary to deliver harsh punishments for the greater good. He took a deep breath and began: "For the sin of theft, you will receive fifty lashes. Should you lose consciousness, the punishment will continue. Should you die, the punishment will continue. Should you live, you will immediately be banished from this place and will never return!"

Jacob licked his lips in anticipation of the blood being spilt. His mouth watered, and he regretted that a good meal would go to waste. The sun had not yet fully risen, but it was light enough for the gathered children to witness the gruesome spectacle that was about to unfold before their eyes. He moved forward for a better view as the first blow was struck. The crowd screamed as blood splashed them. The smell of it drove him forward, lash after brutal lash went in, and Jacob watched silently with cold fury in his eyes, knowing he was the architect of this brutality.

At one point, he almost felt sorry for Paulus before reminding himself of the way he abused and controlled the kids in the orphanage. Paulus was a strong and hard individual, and despite losing consciousness for a few minutes after the flogging, where he remained unmoving and draped over the small cross that served as a whipping post, the yard was eerily quiet after the screams, which were eventually silenced by the lash of the whip. Jacob was conflicted between admiration of Paulus' strength and his murderous hate for him as he began to regain consciousness, groaning pitifully as he did so.

It was sick. It was a disgusting and pathetic sight. A statue of humiliation. Buckets of water were thrown over Paulus in an attempt to revive him fully before he was roughly dragged to his feet. He was given a sack of basic rations and told to leave as he bled and cried; even his victims felt sick after witnessing such a brutal punishment. Jacob, on the other hand, felt alive. He slipped away from the formal banishing speech and made his way to a hillside on the outskirts. He sat and waited. Paulus would have been told to leave Nazareth, and this vantage point allowed Jacob to see which route he would take. He was sure he would go north, as there was a lot of building work available in Sepphoris; he knew this because Josh and his dad often worked up there, and as carpenters, they were usually in demand. *The stone masons had it best, though*, he mused.

He did not have to wait long until a ragged and

desolate figure shuffled into view, his gait wretched and twisted as he tried unsuccessfully to find a way to carry his meagre bag of supplies and walk away from the source of his shame and misery. Jacob watched Paulus pass, his eyes as cold as a hawk that had spotted prey. He watched the broken boy as he struggled on into the desert, lost in his pain, uncertain and stupid. Jacob let him get a mile ahead and noted with satisfaction that no one else had embarked on the route. Everywhere seemed so quiet. Satisfied with the situation, Jacob stood up and casually walked down the hillside to follow his victim. Slowly, he closed the gap, and as he did, he whistled a haunting little tune that he had made up; it had a sad feel to it, which must have held notes from a minor key. Jacob repeated it nonchalantly, drawing out some notes while others were short and punchy. The staccato added texture to the longer, sad and haunting notes.

At first, Paulus, in his broken state, thought he was hearing things, but it soon became impossible to ignore. He turned and saw Jacob following him, slowly drawing closer. The desert was hot and sandy, reaching out to the horizon, and Nazareth was just a dirty smear in the distance. His blood ran cold as Jacob continued to draw closer, his pace slow and inexorable. Paulus tried to run but couldn't. He could barely walk.

"You! You did this to me!" spat Paulus, his voice hoarse and croaky.

"You did it to yourself, darling," Jacob crooned. "I just helped move things in the right direction, like a wolf protecting the sheep."

"What? That doesn't even make sense," retorted Paulus, realising winning the argument was irrelevant and his defiance futile, but continued anyway. "Wolves don't protect sheep!"

"This one does," grinned Jacob wolfishly. "I am going to drink your blood and watch you die today, darling." Jacob said evenly, "But don't worry, I won't let you suffer too long, as I have an appointment at noon."

Horrified, Paulus tried to shuffle off in a hopeless attempt to escape. Jacob let him go, watching him struggle on. He took in the desert expanse and turned 360 degrees. Not a person in sight, excellent. He turned his attention back to Paulus, who had managed to increase the distance between them quite impressively. Everything was so silent, just the slight sound of the wind and the slight gritty crunch of the sand and stone underfoot, regular in rhythm with Jacob's measured pace. *Such a nice change from the constant noise of the orphanage*, Jacob thought.

"Help!" screamed Paulus as Jacob drew closer, his cold eyes displaying no emotion, just animal-like cruelty and calculation.

"Calm down, darling, there is no one to hear your screams. Just me and the vultures," said Jacob, pointing skywards at the circling birds. The path between Nazareth and Sepphoris fed them well. Occasionally, drunken tradesmen returning to Nazareth had reported being attacked by these giant birds who had mistaken them for corpses as they slept off the wine at the side of the road.

"When they find my body, they will know it was you! I told the Director all about you," yelled Paulus. "They will nail you to a cross and leave you out in the desert to die, and then my ghost will come to laugh at you before chasing your wicked soul throughout eternity!"

"You're quite poetic today, darling," smiled Jacob ironically. "They won't find your body, and you will just be bird food," stated Jacob and pointed at the circling vultures again. "Anyway, I'm joining the Roman Army; I'm done with the orphanage."

"You in the Roman Army, don't make me fucking laugh! You're too much of a puss…."

Jacob launched himself forward and delivered a savage elbow strike to Paulus' face. Paulus never saw it coming and never regained consciousness. Jacob drank deeply and grew stronger as a result. He dragged Paulus' body away from the road out into the open, where it was hidden from view in the dead ground and left him for the carrion creatures to devour. Nobody would miss him, and if he were found, Jacob was confident that his demise would be put down to the savage beating he had suffered at the orphanage.

He knew his world had changed, and he was out on his own. *Let's see what the Roman Army has to offer. What was their motto? "Si vis pacem para bellum,"* which translated as, "If you want peace, prepare for war," and Jacob wanted peace. Yet he knew, as the killer he was, that peace would not be part of his future. The Roman Army was his only exit. Jacob trudged back to Nazareth, the desert sun climbing toward noon, his immortal heart steady despite the blood of Paulus still lingering on his tongue, its dark vitality fuelling his steps. He would meet the soldiers at noon as agreed the previous day. When he looked back, he could see that the vultures had already started to land where the remains of the bastard Paulus lay. It was time for a new beginning.

The Centurion and his Optio were waiting by the well, their faces stern but oblivious to the blood on Jacob's hands, his mind already racing with the possibilities of a soldier's life, battles in distant lands, empires to shape, and secrets to guard.

The Optio thrust a wax tablet into Jacob's hands, its surface etched with the stark terms of enlistment, the Centurion's voice a low growl that cut through the Nazareth dust: "Sign here, boy. Glory or a grave awaits. Your selection process begins next week." Jacob's fingers trembled over the stylus, his immortal blood thrumming with a hunger he barely understood. A vision flickered in his mind unbidden: battlefields strewn with fallen kings, thrones crumbling under his shadow, faiths warped by his whispers, a world reshaped in blood across two thousand years. It was gone as swiftly as a dream, leaving only a chill that wasn't the wind. His curse, a blade poised to carve history, stirred within, unknown to him, its edge gleaming with promise, adventure and peril. He pressed the stylus into the wax, his signature a vow to embark on a destiny more sinister and complex than he could have ever imagined.

A Message from the Author

If you enjoyed Genesis of a Vampire, **one of the most powerful ways you can support the series is by leaving a review. You can do this by clicking the link of scanning the QR code below.** Even a sentence or two helps new readers discover the book and keeps this world growing.

Write a Review

Your voice genuinely makes a difference.

Thank you for being part of the journey.

Jon Finn

Join My Mailing List

Step into the shadows of my world. Join the newsletter for exclusive stories, secrets, and adventures you won't find anywhere else.

Get book Two Here

Shadow of the Legions

In the blistering heat of Roman-occupied Judaea, Jacob, an immortal born in the shadow of Christ, has carved out a place for himself among the legions. Once a brutalised orphan, now a rising soldier, he leads his tent group with a predator's instincts and a protector's heart.

But Jerusalem is a city ready to ignite. What begins as routine policing drags Jacob into a hidden world of extortion, trafficking, and blood money, a criminal network thriving under the protection of Rome's most powerful men. Every order he follows reeks of corruption. Every alley hides another secret. And every choice drags him closer to the darkness coiling inside him.

Caught between the fierce compassion of young

Jesus and the cold efficiency demanded by the Roman machine, Jacob walks a razor's edge. He is the wolf among sheep, a creature forged in violence, yet still fighting to hold on to something human.

As the city descends into chaos and loyalties fracture, Jacob must decide what kind of immortal he will become. A soldier who obeys. A monster who hunts. Or something far more dangerous.

The shadows are gathering. And Jacob is done running from them.

Get Book Three Here

Secrets of the Fallen Eagles

After months policing the volatile streets of Jerusalem, Jacob is sent north into a land still haunted by Rome's greatest humiliation. Three years after the disaster in the Teutoburg Forest, the lost eagle standards remain hidden deep within Germania; symbols of Roman shame, and prizes the tribes will kill to keep.

Deployed with a hand-picked unit, Jacob must navigate a world of dense forests, shifting loyalties, and enemies who strike from the shadows but the Germanic warriors are not his only threat. Within the Roman ranks lurks a secret network of soldiers loyal to the tribes men who dream of repeating Arminius' devastating victory and bringing the Empire to its knees.

In a deadly contest of codes, spies, and double agents, Jacob must uncover the traitors before they sabotage the campaign from within. Every message could be a trap. Every ally could be an enemy. And every step deeper into the forest brings him closer to forces determined to see him, and his comrades dead.

Drawing on his instincts and the vampiric abilities he must keep hidden, Jacob wages a silent war of intelligence and survival. To rescue the fallen eagles, he must outwit conspirators, outfight the tribes, and out manoeuvre a foe who knows the terrain far better than Rome ever will.

Secrets of the Fallen Eagles, the third book in the Immortal Conquest series, is written for readers who crave historical adventure sharpened with danger, espionage, and a supernatural edge. It's perfect for those who enjoy gritty Roman military fiction, where loyalty is tested in the mud and blood of the frontier, and every decision can mean life or death.

Get your Copy Here or Scan the QR Code

Tales From Beyond the Forbidden Veil lures you into a shadowy anthology of dark fiction, where secrets pulse beneath the surface. Cunning souls defy death's grasp, only to be ensnared by fates unseen. Enigmatic maps, their lines alive with menace, guide the lost toward realms where danger breathes. A mirror, ancient and omniscient, unveils truths that splinter the mind and romances that transcend mortality itself. Whispers from forgotten ages, etched in dust or carried by spectral voices warn of perils veiled in time. Secrets, long entombed, claw free to unravel destinies.

Across dystopian voids and haunted thresholds, these tales weave dread and mystery, each a riddle wrapped in shadow. Tales From Beyond the Forbidden Veil beckons the bold to peer past the veil, where every story hums with unspoken terrors. For those who crave the uncanny, this collection is a cryptic summons, step closer, but beware: what lies beyond may claim your very soul.

I dare you to read it.

Get Your Copy Here or Scan the QR Code

Step beyond the veil... if you dare.

Tales From the Forbidden Veil 2 is a chilling anthology of dark fiction that plunges you into the uncanny. Inside, cursed portraits reveal evil souls, doppelgängers stalk the living, and forbidden love twists through ancient magic. You'll meet child-snatching fae folk, murderous secret societies, and travellers lost in astral realms. Each tale is a descent into madness, myth, and the forested shadows of the mind where demons whisper and deities judge.

Terrifying, twisted, and wildly imaginative, this collection will haunt your thoughts long after the final

page. It's not just a book - it's a dare.
Go on. Transend the veil. It's waiting.

AFTERWORD

It is undoubtedly an interesting concept to imagine a vampire being born around the same time as Jesus in Jerusalem in the year 6 BC. The adjustments to the Gregorian calendar and the Roman adoption of Christianity under the rule of Emperor Constantine certainly created some theological and chronological conundrums after he converted to Christianity in 312 AD and forced the empire to adopt the Christian religion by building churches on pagan sites. What makes our character truly amazing in this series of books is that he will live, learn and survive over two thousand years of human history.

From being a Jerusalem orphan, he gains experience of the way the world works from his gritty experiences. His eventual understanding of his own immortality dawns slowly as his knowledge of politics, war, and society grows. This is paralleled by his growing understanding of himself and the powers he possesses. "I wish I knew what I know now when I was your age" is a common statement made by older people to their children and colleagues, but imagine how effective you could be if you had lived a thousand lives. This is Jacob. He is a kind but cruel character driven by a sense of justice who is forced to endure the cauldrons of rising and falling empires and a myriad of ever-changing social norms as his loved ones fade away due to their mortality.

On one hand, some may view this as sacrilegious or contradictory to religious beliefs. Vampires are often associated with darkness and evil, while Jesus or Josh is seen as a symbol of light and goodness. The idea of a vampire living during the same time as Jesus may be seen as blasphemous by some.

On the other hand, some may see this as a unique and intriguing twist on the traditional story of Jesus. It could be seen as a metaphor for the constant battle between good and evil, with the vampire representing the darkness and Jesus representing the light. Additionally, it could also prompt discussions about the concept of immortality and what it means to truly live forever. It also raises questions about what happens when our "Light" goes out? How do we fight the darkness?

Perhaps the vampire was a witness to Jesus's teachings and miracles, adding a supernatural element to the stories. In the end, while it may be a controversial and imaginative idea, the concept of a vampire being born in Jerusalem in the year 6 BC opens up discussions about faith, mortality, and the power of storytelling. Jesus was executed by the Romans, and Jacob is still here. He might live right next door to you with all his wisdom and knowledge. I challenge you to think outside the box and consider different perspectives on historical events. Jump in, it's a fantastic journey.

HISTORICAL NOTE

For the purposes of the fluidity of the story, I have made Nazareth much bigger than it originally was. I have also made the Orphanage much bigger. It is highly unlikely that there ever was an orphanage there also, so I just invented one. Most buildings would have been single stories in Nazareth, but the Roman Empire had many multi-storey buildings, so I made the orphanage two stories. Stairways are great for stories. In addition to this, there are stories in The Infancy Gospel of Thomas (IGT), which place Jesus at the death of a child who died falling from a roof, giving some credence to higher buildings of more than one story. It is the intention of this series to take the reader on an epic journey through two thousand years of history using the story of Jacob, the immortal vampire. As he gains the wisdom and knowledge gathered over countless lifetimes, he will be influential in some of the most interesting historical periods and events. As a result, the events of the past will require some poetic licence to allow this. The aim of the books in the Immortal Conquest series is to enjoy the ride and sail the seas of history without getting caught too deeply in the weeds of historical debate.

The Infancy Gospel of Thomas is an intriguing apocryphal text that offers unique insights into the early years of Jesus Christ, detailing events from his fifth to twelfth year. Unlike the canonical gospels, which primarily focus on the adult life and teachings of Jesus, the IGT presents a series of stories that are largely absent from the New Testament, with the exception of the well-known account of Jesus at the Temple found in Luke 2:41–52. It was used to fill out some of the events of the childhood of Jesus and certainly provides some interesting tales contrary to what is written in the official Bible. This is handy when you also have a vampire on the scene at the same time.

The narratives within the IGT depict a remarkable and sometimes controversial portrayal of the young Jesus. Among the episodes, readers encounter not only miraculous healings that foreshadow the miracles of his adulthood but also a range of more troubling incidents. These include instances where Jesus curses or inflicts harm upon those who oppose him, leading to fatalities among those he encounters. Such punishment miracles are a focal point of the text and invite critical reflection on the nature of Jesus during his formative years.

As the stories unfold, a noticeable shift occurs; the more punitive actions attributed to Jesus tend to diminish as he matures. This raises significant questions for scholars: Does this change indicate a personal transformation within Jesus, or does it reflect a changing dynamic in the behaviours and expectations of those around him? The interpretations vary widely, with some scholars suggesting it highlights an early development in Jesus's character while others propose that it reveals more about the societal context of the time.

Additionally, the reception of these narratives among early audiences remains a topic of debate. Did contemporaries view the portrayal of a vengeful Jesus as incongruous with the values of the emerging Christian faith, or have modern sensibilities shaped our understanding of what is deemed "unchristian"? The dialogues surrounding these questions emphasise not only the complexity of the text itself but also the evolving perception of Jesus throughout history.

In sum, The Infancy Gospel of Thomas offers a provocative lens through which to examine the identity of Jesus as a young boy. The duality of his actions, healing and harming, invites readers to ponder deeper theological implications while also reflecting on how perceptions of divinity and morality have transformed over the centuries. This ancient text remains a rich field for exploration, serving as a reminder of the varied and sometimes contradictory narratives that exist in the broader context of Christian writings.

I hope you have enjoyed the beginning of this epic adventure. Any historical mistakes are mine either because the story demands it or because, unlike Jacob, I wasn't there at the time.

ABOUT THE AUTHOR

Jon Finn spent 25 years teaching history before he began writing the story that history forgot to record.

The Immortal Conquest Series is the result of a lifetime's immersion in the ancient world the politics of Rome, the dust of first-century Judea, the battlefield strategies of the legions, and the quieter, stranger stories that exist in the spaces between the history books. When Jon writes about Jacob walking through the streets of Nazareth or navigating the court of a Roman general, the authority in those pages comes from decades of study. No other author in vampire fiction brings that depth of historical knowledge to the genre.

Beyond the classroom, Jon has served in the military, worked across multiple continents, performed in a semi-professional rock band, and drawn on the kind of varied, lived experience that gives his fiction its authenticity. The Immortal Conquest Series currently spans three books. Genesis of a Vampire is available now. Shadow of the Legions is available now. Book Three arrives May 2027. Jacob's story has barely begun.

To find out more and enjoy short, regular stories and upcoming releases, please follow on social media or sign up for newsletters with free advance reader review copies on the website.

Follow me on Facebook and TikTok

@jonfinnauthor

Website

www.jonfinnauthor.com

Email

contact@jonfinnauthor.com